THE DROP

Dennis Lehane

WILLIAM MORROW
An Imprint of HarperCollins*Publishers*

Originally published in a different form, as "Animal Rescue," in the anthology *Boston Noir,* published in 2009 by Akashic Books.

FIRST WILLIAM MORROW PAPERBACK EDITION PUBLISHED 2014.
SECOND WILLIAM MORROW PAPERBACK EDITION PUBLISHED 2021.

The Library of Congress has catalogued a previous edition as follows:

Lehane, Dennis

The drop / Dennis Lehane.—First edition.
    pages cm
"Originally published in a slightly different form in *Boston Noir* in 2009 by Akashic Books"—Title page verso.
ISBN 978-0-06-236544-6 (paperback)
ISBN 978-0-06-236557-6 (hardcover)
1. Criminals—Fiction. 2. Couples—Fiction. 3. Film novelizations.
[1. Rescue dogs—Fiction.] I. Title.
PS3562.E426D76 2014
813'.54—dc23

2014013594

ISBN 978-0-06-308489-6 (pbk.)

21 22 23 24 25   LSC   10 9 8 7 6 5 4 3 2 1

ALSO BY DENNIS LEHANE

A Drink Before the War
Darkness, Take My Hand
Sacred
Gone, Baby, Gone
Prayers for Rain
Mystic River
Shutter Island
Coronado: Stories
The Given Day
Moonlight Mile
Live by Night
World Gone By
Since We Fell

For Tom and Sarah
Now there was a love story.

Meanwhile, "Black sheep, black sheep!" we cry,
Safe in the inner fold;
And maybe they hear, and wonder why,
And marvel, out in the cold.

—RICHARD BURTON, "BLACK SHEEP"

THE DROP

CHAPTER 1

Animal Rescue

BOB FOUND THE DOG two days after Christmas, the neighborhood gone quiet in the cold, hungover and gas-bloated. He was coming off his regular four-to-two shift at Cousin Marv's in the Flats, Bob having worked behind the bar for the better part of two decades now. That night, the bar had been quiet. Millie took up her usual corner stool, nursing a Tom Collins and occasionally whispering to herself or pretending to watch the TV, anything to keep from going back to the seniors home on Edison Green. Cousin Marv, himself, made an appearance and hung around. He claimed to be reconciling the receipts, but mostly he sat in a corner booth in the rear, reading his racing form and texting his sister, Dottie.

They probably would have closed up early if Richie Whelan's friends hadn't commandeered the opposite corner of the bar from Millie and spent the night toasting their long-missing, presumed-dead friend.

Ten years ago to the day, Richie Whelan had left Cousin Marv's to score either some weed or some 'ludes (which was a matter of some debate among his friends) and had never been seen again. Left behind a girlfriend, a kid he never saw who lived with her mother in New Hampshire, and a car in the shop waiting on a new spoiler. That's how everyone knew he was dead; Richie never would have left the car behind; he loved that fucking car.

Very few people called Richie Whelan by his given name. Everyone knew him as Glory Days on account he never shut up about the one year he played QB for East Buckingham High. He led them to a 7–6 record that year, which was hardly newsworthy until you looked at their stats before and since.

So here were long-lost-and-presumed-dead Glory Days' buddies in Cousin Marv's Bar that night—Sully, Donnie, Paul, Stevie, Sean, and Jimmy—watching the Celts get dragged up and down the court by the Heat. Bob brought their fifth round to them unasked and on the house as something happened in the game that caused them all to throw up their hands and groan or shout.

"You're too fucking *old*," Sean yelled at the screen.

Paul said, "They're not that old."

"Rondo just blocked LeBron with his fucking walker," Sean said. "Fucking what's-his-name there, Bogans? He's got an endorsement deal with Depends."

Bob dropped off their drinks in front of Jimmy, the school bus driver.

"You got an opinion on this?" Jimmy asked him.

Bob felt his face pinken, as it often did when people looked directly at him in a way that he felt forced to look directly back. "I don't follow basketball."

Sully, who worked a tollbooth on the Pike, said, "I don't know anything you follow, Bob. You like to read? Watch *The Bachelorette*? Hunt the homeless?"

The boys all chuckled and Bob gave them an apologetic smile.

"Drinks're on the house," he said.

He walked away, tuning out the chatter that followed him.

Paul said, "I've seen chicks—reasonably hot ass—try to chat that guy up, they get nothing."

"Maybe he's into dudes," Sully said.

"Guy ain't into anything."

Sean remembered his manners, raised his drink to Bob and then to Cousin Marv. "Thanks, boys."

Marv, behind the bar now, newspaper spread before him, smiled and raised a glass in acknowledgment, then went back to his paper.

The rest of the guys grabbed their drinks and raised them.

Sean said, "Someone going to say something for the kid?"

Sully said, "To Richie 'Glory Days' Whelan, East Bucky High class of '92, and a funny prick. Rest in peace."

The rest of the guys murmured their approval and drank, and Marv came over to Bob as Bob placed the old glasses in the sink. Marv folded up his paper and took in the guys at the other end of the bar.

"You buy them a round?" he asked Bob.

"They're toasting a dead friend."

"Kid's been dead, what, ten years now?" Marv shrugged his way into the leather car coat he always wore, one that had been in style back when the planes hit the towers in New York City, had been out of style by the time the towers fell. "Gotta be a point where you move on, stop scoring free drinks off the corpse."

Bob rinsed a glass before putting it in the dishwasher, said nothing.

Cousin Marv donned his gloves and scarf, glanced down the other end of the bar at Millie. "Speaking of which, we can't keep letting her ride a stool all night then not pay for her drinks."

Bob put another glass on the upper rack. "She doesn't drink much."

Marv leaned in. "When's the last time you charged her for one, though? And after midnight you let her smoke in here—don't think I don't know. It's not a soup kitchen, it's a bar. She pays her tab tonight or she can't come in until she does."

Bob looked at him, spoke low. "Her tab's like a hundred bucks."

"Hundred-forty actually." Marv worked his way out from the bar, stopped at the door. He pointed at all the holiday decorations on the windows and above the bar. "Oh, and, Bob? Take the Christmas shit down. It's the twenty-seventh."

Bob said, "What about Little Christmas?"

Marv stared at him for a bit. "I don't even know what to say to that," he said and left.

After the Celtics game whimpered to an end like the mercy killing of a relative no one was particularly close to, Richie Whelan's friends shoved off, leaving only old Millie and Bob.

Millie let loose a smoker's cough of limitless phlegm and duration while Bob pushed the broom. Millie continued to cough. Just when it seemed she might choke to death, she stopped.

Bob pushed the broom up by her. "You all right?"

Millie waved him off. "Aces. I'll have one more."

Bob came around behind the bar. He couldn't meet her eyes, so he looked at the black rubber floor covering. "I gotta charge you. I'm sorry. And, Mill'?"—Bob felt like shooting himself in the fucking head he was so embarrassed to be a member of the human race right now—"I gotta settle the tab."

"Oh."

Bob didn't look at her right away. "Yeah."

Millie busied herself with the gym bag she carried out with her every night. "'Course, 'course. You got a business to run. 'Course."

The gym bag was old, the logo on its side faded. She rummaged through it. She placed a dollar bill and sixty-two cents on the bar. Rummaged some more, came back with an antique picture frame with no picture in it. She lay it on the bar.

"That's sterling silver from Water Street Jewelers," Millie said. "RFK bought a watch for Ethel there, Bob. That's worth bucks."

Bob said, "You don't keep a picture in there?"

Millie looked off at the clock above the bar. "It faded."

"Of you?" Bob asked.

Millie nodded. "And the kids."

She looked back into her bag, rummaged some more. Bob put an ashtray in front of her. She looked up at him. He wanted to pat her hand—a gesture of comfort, of you-are-not-entirely-alone—but gestures like that were better left to other people, people in the movies, maybe. Every time Bob tried something personal like that, it came off awkward.

So, he turned and made her another drink.

He brought the drink to her. He took the dollar off the bar and turned back toward the register.

Millie said, "No, take the—"

Bob looked back over his shoulder at her. "This'll cover it."

Bob bought his clothes at Target—new T-shirts, jeans, and flannels about every two years; he drove a Chevy Impala he'd had since his father had handed him the keys in 1983, and the speedometer had yet to find the 100K mark because he never drove anywhere; his house was paid for, the property taxes a joke because, shit, who wanted to live here? So if there was one thing

Bob had that few would have guessed he had it was disposable income. He put the dollar bill in the drawer. He reached into his pocket, pulled out a roll of bills, and held it in front of him as he peeled off seven twenties and added them to the drawer.

When he turned back, Millie had swept the change and the picture frame back into her gym bag.

Millie drank and Bob finished cleaning up, came back around the bar as she was rattling the ice cubes in her glass.

"You ever hear of Little Christmas?" he asked her.

"'Course," she said. "January sixth."

"Nobody remembers it anymore."

"Meant something in my time," she said.

"My old man's too."

Her voice picked up a tone of distracted pity. "Not yours, though."

"Not mine," Bob agreed and felt a trapped bird flutter in his chest, helpless, looking for a way out.

Millie took a huge drag off her cigarette and exhaled with relish. She coughed a few more times and put out her smoke. She put on a raggedy winter coat and ambled to the door. Bob opened it to a light snowfall.

"'Night, Bob."

"Careful out there," Bob said. "Watch the ice."

THIS YEAR, THE TWENTY-EIGHTH was trash day in his section of the Flats, and people had long since put their barrels to the curb for the morning pickup. Bob trekked the sidewalks toward home, noting with a mix of amusement and despair what people threw out. So many toys so quickly broken. So many discards of things that worked perfectly fine but had been designated for replacement. Toasters, TVs, microwaves, stereo equipment, clothing, remote-controlled cars and planes and monster trucks that only required a little glue here, a strip of tape there. And it wasn't as if his neighbors were wealthy. Bob couldn't count how many domestic squabbles over money had kept him up at night, had lost track of all the faces who climbed on the subway in the morning and sagged with worry, Help Wanted pages clutched in sweaty fists. He stood behind them in line at Cottage Market as they thumbed through their food stamps and in the bank as they cashed their SSI checks. Some worked two jobs, some could only afford housing through Section 8 allowances, and some studied the sorrow of their lives at Cousin Marv's, eyes gone far away, fingers clutching their mug handles.

And yet they acquired. They built scaffolds of debt, and just when it seemed the pile would come tumbling down from the weight, they bought a living room set on layaway, tossed it up on top. And as they needed to acquire, they seemed to need to discard in equal or larger measure. There was an almost violent addiction in the piles of trash he saw, the sense it gave him of shitting out food you shouldn't have eaten in the first place.

Bob—excluded from even this ritual by his mark of

loneliness, his inability to draw anyone to him who seemed interested in him beyond five minutes of topic-of-the-day conversation—sometimes gave into the sin of pride on these walks, pride that he himself did not consume recklessly, felt no need to purchase what they demand he purchase on TV and radio and billboards and in magazines and newspapers. It would bring him no closer to what he wanted because all he wanted was to not be alone, but he knew there was no getting rescued from that.

He lived alone in the house he grew up in, and when it seemed likely to swallow him with its smells and memories and dark couches, the attempts he'd made to escape it—through church socials, lodge picnics, and one horrific mixer thrown by a dating service—had only opened the wound farther, left him patching it back up for weeks, cursing himself for hoping. Stupid hope, he'd sometimes whisper to his living room. Stupid, stupid hope.

But it lived in him, nonetheless. Quietly, even hopelessly most times. Hopeless hope, he'd think sometimes and manage a smile, people on the subway wondering what the hell Bob was smiling about. Odd, lonely Bob the bartender. Nice enough guy, can be depended on to help shovel a walk or buy a round, a good guy, but so shy you couldn't hear what he was saying half the time, so you gave up, tossed him a polite nod, and turned to someone else.

Bob knew what they said, and he couldn't blame them. He could step outside himself enough to see what they saw—a

never-was loser, ill at ease in social situations, given to stray
nervous tics like blinking too much for no reason and cocking
his head at odd angles when he was daydreaming, kinda guy
made the other losers look a little brighter in comparison.

"You have so much love in your heart," Father Regan said
to Bob the time Bob broke down crying in confession. Father Regan took him back into the sacristy and they shared a
couple glasses of the single malt the priest kept tucked away
on a closet shelf above the cassocks. "You do, Bob. It's plain
for everyone to see. And I can't help but believe some good
woman, some woman with faith in God, will see that love
and run to it."

How to tell a man of God about the world of man? Bob
knew the priest meant well, knew that he was right in theory.
But experience had shown Bob that women saw the love in
his heart, all right, they just preferred a heart with a more
attractive casing around it. And it wasn't just the women, it
was *him*. Bob didn't trust himself around breakable things.
Hadn't in years.

That night, he paused on the sidewalk, feeling the ink sky
above him and the cold in his fingers, and he closed his eyes
against the evening.

He was used to it. He was used to it.

It was okay.

You could make a friend of it, as long as you didn't fight it.

With his eyes closed, he heard it—a worn-out keening
accompanied by distant scratching and a sharper, metallic rat-

tling. He opened his eyes. A large metal barrel with a heavy lid clamped tight on top. Fifteen feet down the sidewalk on the right. It shook slightly under the yellow glare of the streetlight, its bottom scraping the sidewalk. He stood over it and heard that keening again, the sound of a creature that was one breath away from deciding it was too hard to take the next, and Bob pulled off the lid.

He had to remove some things to get to it—a doorless microwave and five thick Yellow Pages, the oldest dating back to 2005, piled atop some soiled bedding and musty pillows. The dog—either a very small one or else a puppy—was down at the bottom, and it scrunched its head into its midsection when the light hit it. It exhaled a soft chug of a whimper and tightened its body even more, its eyes closed to slits. A scrawny thing. Bob could see its ribs. He could see a big crust of dried blood by its ear. No collar. It was brown with a white snout and paws that seemed far too big for its body.

It let out a sharper whimper when Bob reached down, sank his fingers into the nape of its neck, and lifted it out of its own excrement. Bob didn't know dogs too well, but there was no mistaking this one for anything but a boxer. And definitely a puppy, the wide brown eyes opening and looking into his as he held it up before him.

Somewhere, he was sure, two people made love. A man and a woman. Entwined. Behind one of those shades, oranged with light, that looked down on the street. Bob could feel them in there, naked and blessed. And he stood out here in the cold with a near-dead dog staring back at him. The icy sidewalk glinted like new marble, and the wind was dark and gray as slush.

"What do you got there?"

Bob turned, looked up and down the sidewalk.

"I'm up here. And you're in my trash."

She stood on the front porch of the three-decker nearest him. She'd turned the porch light on and stood there shivering, her feet bare. She reached into the pocket of her hoodie and came back with a pack of cigarettes. She watched him as she got one going.

"I've got a dog." Bob held it up.

"A *what*?"

"A dog. A puppy. A boxer, I think."

She coughed out some smoke. "Who puts a dog in a barrel?"

"I know," he said. "Right? It's bleeding." He took a step toward her stairs and she backed up.

"Who do you know that I would know?" A city girl, not about to just drop her guard around a stranger.

"I don't know," Bob said. "How about Francie Hedges?"

She shook her head. "You know the Sullivans?"

That wouldn't narrow it down. Not around here. You shook a tree, a Sullivan fell out. Followed by a six-pack most times. "I know a bunch."

This was going nowhere, the puppy looking at him, shaking worse than the girl.

"Hey," she said, "you live in this parish?"

"Next one over." He tilted his head to the left. "Saint Dom's."

"Go to church?"

"Most Sundays."

"So you know Father Pete?"

"Pete Regan," he said, "sure."

She produced a cell phone. "What's your name?"

"Bob," he said. "Bob Saginowski."

She raised her cell phone and took his picture. He hadn't even known it was happening or he at least would have run a hand through his hair.

Bob waited as she stepped back from the light, phone to one ear, finger pressed into the other. He stared at the puppy. The puppy stared back, like, How did I get *here*? Bob touched its nose with his index finger. The puppy blinked its huge eyes. For a moment, Bob couldn't recall his sins.

"That picture just went out," she said from the darkness. "To Father Pete and six other people."

Bob stared into the darkness, said nothing.

"Nadia," the girl said and stepped back into the light. "Bring him up here, Bob."

THEY WASHED IT IN Nadia's sink, dried it off, and brought it to her kitchen table.

Nadia was small. A bumpy rope of a scar ran across the

base of her throat. It was dark red, the smile of a drunk circus clown. She had a tiny moon of a face, savaged by pockmarks, and small, heart-pendant eyes. Shoulders that didn't cut so much as dissolve at the arms. Elbows like flattened beer cans. A yellow bob of hair curled on either side of her oval face. "It's not a boxer." Her eyes glanced off Bob's face before dropping the puppy back onto her kitchen table. "It's an American Staffordshire terrier."

Bob knew he was supposed to understand something in her tone, but he didn't know what that thing was, so he remained silent.

She glanced back up at him after the quiet lasted too long. "A pit bull."

"That's a pit bull?"

She nodded and swabbed the puppy's head wound again. Someone had pummeled it, she'd told Bob. Probably knocked it unconscious, assumed it was dead, and dumped it.

"Why?" Bob said.

She looked at him, her round eyes getting rounder, wider. "Just because." She shrugged, went back to examining the dog. "I worked at Animal Rescue once. You know the place on Shawmut? As a vet tech? Before I decided it wasn't my thing. They're so hard, this breed . . ."

"What?"

"To adopt out," she said. "It's very hard to find them a home."

"I don't know about dogs. I never had a dog. I live alone.

I just was walking by the barrel." Bob found himself beset by a desperate need to explain himself, explain his life. "I'm just not . . ." He could hear the wind outside, black and rattling. Rain or bits of hail spit against the windows. Nadia lifted the puppy's back left paw—the other three paws were brown, but this one was white with peach spots. She dropped the paw as if it were contagious. She went back to the head wound, took a closer look at the right ear, a piece missing from the tip that Bob hadn't noticed until now.

"Well," she said, "he'll live. You're gonna need a crate and food and all sorts of stuff."

"No," Bob said. "You don't understand."

She cocked her head, gave him a look that said she understood perfectly.

"I can't. I just found him. I was gonna give him back."

"To whoever beat him, left him for dead?"

"No, no, like, the authorities."

"That would be Animal Rescue," she said. "After they give the owner seven days to reclaim him, they'll—"

"The guy who beat him? He gets a second chance?"

She gave him a half frown and a nod. "*If* he doesn't take it"—she lifted the puppy's ear, peered in—"chances are this little fella'll be put up for adoption. But it's hard. To find them a home. Pit bulls. More often than not?" She looked at Bob. "More often than not, they're put down."

Bob felt a wave of sadness roll out from her that immediately shamed him. He didn't know how, but he'd caused pain. He'd put some out into the world. He'd let this girl down. "I . . ." he started. "It's just . . ."

She glanced up at him. "I'm sorry?"

Bob looked at the puppy. Its eyes were droopy from a long day in a barrel and whoever gave it that wound. It had stopped shivering, though.

"You can take it," Bob said. "You used to work there, like you said. You—"

She shook her head. "I can't even take care of myself." She shook her head again. "And I work too much. Crazy hours, too. Unpredictable."

"Can you give me 'til Sunday morning?" Bob wasn't sure how it was the words left his mouth, since he couldn't remember formulating them or even thinking them.

The girl eyed him carefully. "You're not just saying it? 'Cause, I shit you not, he ain't picked up by Sunday noon, he's back out that door."

"Sunday, then." Bob said the words with a conviction he actually felt. "Sunday definitely."

"Yeah?"

"Yeah." Bob felt crazed. He felt light as a communion wafer. "Yeah."

CHAPTER 2

Infinite

THE DAILY 7:00 AM mass at Saint Dominic's hadn't drawn a crowd since before Bob was born. But now the numbers, always grim, dwindled by the month.

The morning after he found the dog, he could hear the hem of Father Regan's cassock brush the marble floor of the altar from the tenth row. The only people in attendance that morning—a bitter one, to be sure, black ice all over the streets, wind so cold you could nearly see it—were Bob; Widow Malone; Theresa Coe, once the principal of Saint Dom's School, when there was a Saint Dom's School; Old Man Williams; and the Puerto Rican cop, whose name, Bob was pretty sure, was Torres.

Torres didn't look like a cop—his eyes were kind, sometimes even playful—so it could be surprising to notice the holster on his hip when he turned into his pew after Communion. Bob, himself, never took Communion, a fact not lost on Father Regan, who'd tried several times to convince him that the damage done by not taking the Eucharist, if he were, in fact, in a state of mortal sin, was far worse, in the good priest's opinion, than the damage that could be wrought by partaking of the sacrament. Bob, however, had been raised old school Catholic, back when you heard a lot about Limbo and even more about Purgatory, back when nuns reigned with punitive rulers. So even though Bob, theologically speaking, leaned left on most Church teachings, he remained a traditionalist.

Saint Dom's was an older church. Dated back to the late 1800s. A beautiful building—dark mahogany and off-white marble, towering stained glass windows dedicated to various sad-eyed saints. It looked the way a church should look. The newer churches—Bob didn't know what to do with them. The pews were too blond, the skylights too numerous. They made him feel like he was there to revel in his life, not ruminate on his sins.

But in an old church, a church of mahogany and marble and dark wainscoting, a church of quiet majesty and implacable history, he could properly reflect on both his hopes and his transgressions.

The other parishioners lined up to receive the host while

Bob remained kneeling in his pew. There was no one around him. He was an island.

The cop Torres was up there now, a good-looking guy in his early forties, going a bit doughy. He took the host on his tongue, not in a cupped palm. A traditionalist too.

He turned, blessing himself, and his eyes skipped across Bob's before he reached his pew.

"All rise."

Bob blessed himself and stood. He lifted the kneeler back into place with his foot.

Father Regan raised his hand above the throng and closed his eyes. "May the Lord bless you and keep you all the days of your lives. May He make His face shine upon you and be gracious to you. May the Lord lift up His face upon you and give you peace. This mass has ended. Go in peace to love and serve the Lord. Amen."

Bob exited his pew and walked down the aisle. At the holy water font by the exit, he dipped his fingers and blessed himself. At the next font over, Torres did the same. Torres nodded hello, one familiar stranger to another. Bob returned the nod and they took separate exits out into the cold.

BOB WENT INTO WORK at Cousin Marv's around noon because he liked it when it was quiet. Gave him time to think over this puppy proposition he was facing.

Most people called Marv Cousin Marv out of habit, something that went back to grade school, though no one could remember why, but Marv actually was Bob's cousin. On their mothers' side.

Cousin Marv had run a crew in the late 1980s and early 1990s. It had been primarily comprised of guys with interests in the loaning and subsequent debt-repayment side of things, though Marv never turned his nose down at any paying proposition because he believed, to the core of his soul, that those who failed to diversify were always the first to collapse when the wind turned. Like the dinosaurs, he'd say to Bob, when the cavemen came along and invented arrows. Picture the cavemen, he'd say, firing away, and the tyrannosauruses all gucked up in the oil puddles. A tragedy so easily averted.

Marv's crew hadn't been the toughest crew or the smartest or the most successful operating in the neighborhood— not even close—but for a while they got by. Other crews kept nipping at their heels, though, and except for one glaring exception, they'd never been ones to favor violence. Pretty soon, they had to make the decision to yield to crews a lot meaner than they were or duke it out. They took Door Number One.

Marv was a fence now, one of the best in the city, but a fence in their world was like a mailroom clerk in the straight world—if you were still doing it after thirty, it was all you'd ever do. Marv also took some bets, but only for Chovka's father and the rest of the Chechens who really owned this bar. It wasn't exactly common knowledge, though it was no secret, that Cousin Marv hadn't owned Cousin Marv's outright for years.

For Bob, it was a relief—he liked being a bartender and he'd hated that one time they'd had to come heavy. Marv, though, Marv still waited for the diamond-crusted train to arrive on the eighteen-karat tracks, take him away from all this. Most times, he pretended to be happy. But Bob knew that the things that haunted Marv were the same things that haunted Bob—the shitty things you did to get ahead. Those things laughed at you if your ambitions failed to amount to much; a successful man could hide his past, but an unsuccessful man spent the rest of his life trying not to drown in his.

That afternoon, Marv was looking a hair on the mournful side, so Bob tried to cheer him up by telling him about his adventure with the dog. Marv didn't seem too interested, but Bob kept trying as he spread ice melt in the alley and Marv smoked by the back door.

"Make sure you get it everywhere," Marv said. "All I need, one of those Cape Verdeans slips on the way to the Dumpster."

"What Cape Verdeans?"

"The ones in the hair place."

"The nail place? They're Vietnamese."

"Well, I don't want 'em slipping."

Bob said, "You know a Nadia Dunn?"

Marv shook his head.

"She's the one holding the dog."

Marv said, "This dog again."

Bob said, "Training a dog, you know? Housebreaking? It's a lot of responsibility."

Cousin Marv flicked his cigarette into the alley. "It's not like some long-lost retard relative, shows up at your door in a wheelchair with a colostomy bag, says he's yours now. It's a dog."

Bob said, "Yeah, but . . ." and couldn't find the words to express something he'd felt since he'd first lifted the puppy out of the barrel and stared into its eyes, that for the first time he could ever recall, he felt like he was starring in the movie of his own life, not just sitting in the back row of a noisy theater watching it.

Cousin Marv patted his shoulder, leaned in reeking of smoke, and repeated himself. "It's. A. Dog." And then he walked back into the bar.

AROUND THREE, ANWAR, ONE of Chovka's guys, came in through the back for last night's book. Chovka's guys were running late on pickups all over the city because the BPD had dropped a little harassment raid down on the Chechen social club last night, put half the runners and bagmen in jail for the night. Anwar took the bag Marv handed over and helped himself to a Stella. He drank it in one long, slow pull as he eye-fucked Marv and Bob. When he finished, he burped, put the bottle back on the bar, and left without a word, the bag of money under his arm.

"No respect." Marv dumped the bottle and wiped up the ring it had left on the bar. "You notice?"

Bob shrugged. Of course he noticed, but what were you going to do?

"This puppy, right?" he said to lighten the mood. "He's got paws the size of his head. Three are brown but one's white with these little peach-colored spots over the white. And—"

"This thing cook?" Marv said. "Clean the house? I mean, it's a fucking dog."

"Yeah, but it was—" Bob dropped his hands. He didn't know how to explain. "You know that feeling you get sometimes on a really great day? Like, like, the Pats dominate and you took the 'over,' or they cook your steak just right up the Blarney or, or, you just feel *good*? Like"—Bob found himself waving his hands again—"good?"

Marv gave him a nod and a tight smile. Went back to his racing sheet.

Bob alternated between taking down the Christmas decorations and working the bar, but the place started to fill after five, and pretty soon it was all bartending all the time. By this point, Rardy, the other bartender, should have been pitching in, but he was late.

Bob made two trips to run a round over to a dozen guys by the dartboards who laid fiber-optic cable in all the hotels springing up down the Seaport. He came back behind the bar, found Marv leaning against a beer cooler, reading the

Herald, but the customers blamed Bob for the slowdown, one guy asking if his Buds were coming by fucking Clydesdales.

Bob nudged Marv aside, reached in the cooler, and mentioned Rardy was late. Again. Bob, who'd never been late in his life, suspected there was something hostile at the core of people who always were.

Marv said, "No, he's here," and gestured with his head. Bob could see the kid now, Rardy about thirty but still getting carded at the door to a club. Rardy, chatting up customers as he worked his way through the crowd in his faded hoodie and battered jeans, porkpie hat resting on the crown of his head, always looking like he was on his way to open mic night for either poetry or stand-up. Bob had known him for five years now, though, and he knew Rardy didn't possess an ounce of sensitivity and couldn't tell a joke for shit.

"Yo," the kid said when he got behind the bar. He took his time removing his jacket. "Cavalry's here." He slapped Bob on the back. "Lucky for you, right?"

OUTSIDE IN THE COLD, two brothers drove past the bar for the third time that day, looping around back through the alley, and then out onto Main, where they headed away from the bar so they could find a parking lot to do another couple of lines.

Their names were Ed and Brian Fitzgerald. Ed was older and overweight and everyone called him Fitz. Brian was thinner than a tongue depressor and everyone called him Bri. Except when they were referred to as a pair, in which case some folks called them "10" because that's pretty much what they looked like when they stood side by side.

Fitz had the ski masks in the backseat and the guns in the trunk. He kept the blow in the console between the two seats. Bri needed the blow. Otherwise, he'd never go near a fucking gun.

They found an isolated spot under the expressway. From there they could see Penitentiary Park, covered in crusts of ice and rags of snow. From where they were sitting, they could even see the spot where the drive-in screen had once stood. A few years before it was torn down, a girl had been found beaten to death there, probably the neighborhood's most famous murder. Fitz cut their lines on a glass square he'd popped out of the side-view mirror of a junker. He snorted the first bump, handed the mirror and the rolled-up fin to his brother.

Bri snorted his bump and then didn't even ask before he snorted the one next to it.

"I don't know," Bri said, which he'd been saying so much this week Fitz was going to fucking strangle him if he kept it up. "I don't know."

Fitz took the rolled-up fin and the mirror back. "It's gonna be fine."

"No," Bri said. He fiddled with his watch, which had stopped keeping time a year ago. A parting gift from their father the day he decided he didn't want to be a father anymore. "It's a bad fucking idea. Just bad. We should hit them for everything or not at all."

"My guy," Fitz explained for maybe the fiftieth time, "wants to see we can handle our shit. Says we do it in steps. See how the owners react the first time."

Bri's eyes grew wide. "They could respond real fucking bad, you nut. That's a fucking gangsta bar. A drop bar."

Fitz gave him a tight smile. "That's kinda the point. If it wasn't a drop bar, it would never be worth the risk."

"No. All right?" Bri kicked the underside of the glove compartment. A child throwing a tantrum. He fiddled with the watch again, turning the band so that the face of the watch found the inside of his wrist. "No, no, no."

Fitz said, "No? Little brother, you got Ashley, the kids, and a fucking habit. Your car's been nursing the same tank of gas since Thanksgiving and your watch still don't fucking work." He leaned across the car until his forehead touched his little brother's. He put his hand on the back of his neck. "Say 'no' again."

Bri didn't, of course. Instead, he did another line.

IT WAS A BIG night, lots of Buds and lots of bets going down. Bob and Rardy handled the former. Marv took care of the itchy, and always slightly bewildered, bettors and dropped the bets into the slot in the cabinet below the register. At some point, he disappeared into the back to tally it all up, came out after the crowd had thinned considerably.

Bob was skimming the foam off two pints of Guinness when two Chechens came through the door with their close-cropped hair, two days' beard growth, wearing silk warm-up jackets under woolen topcoats. Marv passed them and handed off the manila envelope without breaking stride, and by the time Bob had skimmed the rest of the foam off the pints, the Chechens were gone. In and out. Like they were never there.

An hour later, the place was empty. Bob mopped up behind the bar, Marv counted the revenue. Rardy dragged the trash out the back door into the alley. Bob squeezed the mop out in the bucket, and when he looked up there was a guy standing in the rear doorway pointing a shotgun at him.

The thing he'd always remember about it, for the rest of his life, was the quiet. How the rest of the world was asleep—inside, outside—and all was still. And yet a man stood in the doorway with a ski mask over his head and a shotgun pointed at Bob and Marv.

Bob dropped his mop.

Marv, standing by one of the beer coolers, looked up. His eyes narrowed. Just below his hand was a 9mm Glock. And Bob hoped to God he wasn't stupid enough to reach for it. That shotgun would cut them both in half before Marv's hand cleared the bar.

But Marv was no fool. Very slowly, he raised his hands

above his shoulders before the guy could even tell him to, so Bob did the same.

The guy stepped into the room and Bob got a sick feeling in his chest when another guy came in behind the first one, pointing a revolver at them, that guy's hand shaking just a bit. It had somehow been manageable when there'd only been one guy with a gun, but with two of them the bar grew as tight as a swollen blister. All it needed was the pin. This could be the end, Bob realized. Five minutes from now—or even thirty seconds—he could learn if there was a life after this one or just the pain of steel penetrating his body and rupturing his organs. Followed by nothing.

The guy with the shaky hand was thin, the guy with the shotgun was beefy, actually fat, and they both breathed heavily through the ski masks. The thin guy put a kitchen trash bag on the bar, but it was the overweight guy who did the talking.

He said to Marv, "Don't even think, just fill it."

Marv nodded like he was taking the guy's drink order and began moving the cash he'd just rubber-banded into the bag.

"I'm not trying to make trouble," Marv said.

"Well, you're fucking making it," the big guy said.

Marv stopped putting the money in the bag and looked over at him. "But do you know whose bar this is? Whose money you're actually jacking here?"

The thin one stepped in close with the shaky gun. "Fill the bag, you fucking goof."

The thin one wore a watch on his right wrist with the face turned in. Bob noticed it read six-fifteen even though it was half past two in the morning.

"No worries," Marv said to the shaking gun. "No worries." And he put the rest of the money in the bag.

The thin guy clutched the bag to him and stepped back and now it was the two of them on one side of the bar with their guns and Bob and Marv on the other side, Bob's heart beating in his chest like a sack of ferrets tossed off a boat.

In that terrible moment, Bob felt all time since the birth of the world opening its mouth for him. He could see the night sky expanding into space and space expanding into infinite space with stars hurled across the black sky like diamonds on felt, and it was all just cold and endless and he was less than a mote in it. He was the memory of a mote, the memory of something that had passed through unnoticed. The memory of something not worth remembering.

I just want to raise the dog, he thought for some reason. I just want to teach it tricks and live more of this life.

The thin guy pocketed his pistol and walked out.

Now there was just the big guy and that shotgun.

He said to Marv, "You fucking talk too much."

And then he was gone.

The door to the alley squeaked when they opened it, squeaked when it closed again. Bob didn't take a breath for at least half a minute and then he and Marv exhaled at the same time.

Bob heard a low sound, a kind of moan, but it wasn't Marv making it.

"Rardy," Bob said.

"Ho shit." Marv came around the bar with him and they ran through the tiny kitchen into the back where they stored the old kegs, and there was Rardy, lying on his stomach to the left of the door, face caked in blood.

Bob wasn't sure what to do, but Marv dropped down by him and began yanking his shoulder back and forth like it was the string to an outboard motor. Rardy groaned a few times and then he gasped. It was a horrible sound, all strangled and broken, like he was inhaling broken glass. He arched his back and rolled onto his side and then sat up, his face stretched against the skull, his lips pulled back against his teeth like some kind of death mask.

"Oh," he said, "my fuck. My fuck. God."

He opened his eyes for the first time, and Bob watched him try to focus. It took a minute.

"What the *fuck*?" he said, which Bob thought was a step up from "my fuck," if anyone was wondering about the brain damage issue.

"You all right?" Bob asked.

"Yeah, you okay?" Marv stood up beside Bob, both of them bending at the knees by Rardy.

"I'm gonna puke."

Bob and Marv took a few steps back.

Rardy let out several shallow breaths, took in several shal-

low breaths, exhaled another round of them, and then announced, "No, I'm not."

Bob took a couple steps forward. Marv hung back.

Bob handed Rardy a kitchen towel and Rardy touched it
to the jellyfish of blood and raw flesh that covered the right
side of his face from his eye socket to the corner of his mouth.

"How bad do I look?"

"You look okay," Bob lied.

"Yeah, you look good," Marv said.

"No, I don't," Rardy said.

"No, you don't," Bob and Marv agreed.

CHAPTER 3

Drop Bar

Two patrolwomen, Fenton, G., and Bernardo, R., responded to the call first. They took one look at Rardy, and R. Bernardo keyed her shoulder mike and told dispatch to send an ambulance. They questioned all three of them but focused on Rardy because no one figured he'd last long. His skin was the color of November and he kept licking his lips and blinking his eyelids. If he'd never had a concussion before, he could check it off the list now.

Then the door opened and the lead detective came in, his blank, disinterested face growing curious and then amused as his eyes landed on Bob.

He pointed at him. "The seven at Saint Dom's."

Bob nodded. "Yeah."

"Every morning we see each other for, what now, two years? Three? And we've never met." He held out his hand. "Detective Evandro Torres."

Bob shook his hand. "Bob Saginowski."

Detective Torres shook Marv's hand too. "Let me talk to my girls—wait, my officers, excuse me—and then we'll all go over what happened."

He walked a few paces to Officers Fenton and Bernardo and they all spoke in low tones and nodded and pointed a lot.

Marv said, "You know the guy?"

"Don't know him," Bob said. "He goes to the same mass."

"What's he like?"

Bob shrugged. "Don't know."

"He goes to the same church, you don't know what he's like?"

"You know all the regulars you see at the gym?"

"That's different."

"How?"

Marv sighed. "It just is."

Torres came back, all pearly white teeth and playful eyes. He had them tell him in their own words exactly what they remembered, and their stories were pretty identical although they disagreed about whether the one with the pistol had called Marv a "goof" or a "fuck." Otherwise, though, they were in sync. They left out the entire part about Marv asking the chunky guy if he knew whose bar this really was and yet they'd never had time to consult each other on the issue. But around East Buckingham, the maternity ward at Saint Margaret's Hospital had the words KEEP YOUR FUCKING MOUTH SHUT scrawled above the entrance.

Torres scribbled away in his reporter's notebook. "So, I mean, ski masks, black turtlenecks under black coats, black jeans, the skinny one more nervous than the other one, both of them pretty cool under pressure, though. Nothing else you remember?"

"That's about it," Marv said, turning on his helpful smile. Mr. Well Meaning.

"Guy closest to me," Bob said, "his watch was stopped."

He felt Marv's eyes on him, saw Rardy, an ice bag to his face, look over too. For the life of him, he had no idea why he'd opened his mouth. And then, even more to his surprise, he kept fucking talking.

"He wore the face turned in like this." Bob turned his wrist up.

Torres held his pen poised over the paper. "And the hands were stopped?"

Bob nodded. "Yeah. At six-fifteen."

Torres made note of that. "How much they take you for?"

Marv said, "Whatever was in the register."

Torres kept his eyes and his smile on Bob. "*Just* what was in the register?"

Bob said, "Whatever was in the register, Officer."

"Detective."

"Detective. Just what was in there."

Torres looked around the bar a bit. "So if I was to ask around, I wouldn't hear anything about anyone making book here or, I dunno"— he looked at Marv—"providing safe passage for purloined items?"

"Fucking *what* items?"

"Purloined," Torres said. "It's a pretty word for stolen."

Marv acted like he was giving it some thought. Then he shook his head.

Torres looked at Bob, and he shook his head too.

"Or moving a bag of weed every now and then?" Torres said. "I wouldn't hear nothing about that?"

Marv and Bob embraced the Fifth without actually invoking it.

Torres rocked back on his heels, taking them both in like they were a comedy skit. "And when I go through your register tapes—Rita, make sure you grab those, 'kay?—they'll line up exactly with the amount of money got took?"

"Absolutely," Marv said.

"You bet," Bob said.

Torres laughed. "Ah, so the bagmen already came by. Lucky for you."

It finally got to Marv and he scowled. "I don't like what you're, you know, insinuating. We got robbed."

"I know you got robbed."

"But you're treating us like suspects."

"Not for robbing your own bar, though." Torres gave Marv

a soft roll of the eyes and a sigh. "Marv—it's Marv, right?"

Marv nodded. "That's what the sign above the building says, yeah."

"Okay, Marv." Torres patted Marv's elbow and Bob got the feeling he was trying not to smirk. "Everyone knows you're a drop."

"A what?" Marv put his hand behind his ear, leaned in.

"A drop," Torres said. "A drop bar."

"I am not familiar with that term," Marv said, looking around for a peanut gallery to play to.

"No?" Torres played along, enjoying himself. "Well, let's just say this neighborhood and a couple others around the city, they got a criminal element."

"Hush your mouth," Marv said.

Torres's eyes widened. "Oh, no, I'm serious. And so the rumor—some call it urban legend, others call it fucking fact, excuse my French—the rumor is that a criminal collective, a syndicate if you will—"

Marv laughed. "A syndicate!"

Torres laughed too. "Right? Yeah, a criminal syndicate, yes, made up mostly of Eastern Europeans, those would be your Croatians and Russians and Chechens and Ukrainians—"

"What, no Bulgarians?" Marv said.

"Them too," Torres said. "So the rumor is— You ready?"

"I'm ready," Marv said, and it was his turn to rock back on his heels.

"The rumor is that this syndicate takes bets and does drug sales and runs hookers all over the city. I mean, east to west and north to south. But every time we in the police try to bust those illicit gains, as we call them, the money isn't where we thought it was." Torres held up his hands in surprise.

Marv mocked the gesture, adding a sad clown face for good measure.

"Where's the money?"

"Where?" Marv wondered.

"It's not in the whorehouse, it's not in the drug den, not at the bookie's joint. It's gone."

"Poof."

"Poof," Torres agreed. He lowered his voice and gathered Bob and Marv to him. He spoke in a voice so low it was almost a whisper. "The theory is that every night, all the money is collected and"—he made air quotes with his fingers—"'dropped' in a preselected bar somewhere in the city. The bar takes all the money from all the illegal shit going on in the city that night and sits on it until the morning. And then some Russian in a black leather trench coat and too much aftershave shows up, takes the money, and runs it back across the city to the syndicate."

"This syndicate again," Marv said.

"And that's it." Torres clapped his hands together so sharply that Rardy looked over. "Money gone."

"Can I ask you something?" Marv said.

"Sure."

"Why not just sit on the bar in question with a warrant and bust them for receiving all that illegal money?"

"Ah," Torres said, holding up his index finger. "Great idea. You ever think about becoming a cop?"

"Nah."

"You sure? You got a knack for this, Marv."

"I'm just a humble publican."

Torres chuckled and leaned in again, all conspiratorial. "The reason we can't bust a drop bar is that no one, not even the drop bar, *knows* it's gonna be the drop bar until a few hours before it happens."

"*No.*"

"*Yes.* And then it might not be the drop bar for six months. Or it might be called into action two days later. Point is—you never know."

Marv scratched his stubble. "You never know," he repeated with soft wonder.

The three of them just stood there for a bit, nothing to say.

"Well, you think of anything else," Torres finally said, "you give me a call." He handed each of them his card.

"Chances of catching these guys?" Marv fanned his face with the card.

"Oh," Torres said magnanimously, "slim."

"At least you're honest."

"At least one of us is." Torres laughed sharp and loud.

Marv joined him and then cut it off abruptly, let his eyes ice over like he was still a hard guy.

Torres looked at Bob. "Shame about Saint Dom's, ain't it?"

"What about it?" Bob asked, happy to talk about something—anything—else.

"It's gone, Bob. They're closing their doors."

Bob's mouth opened but he couldn't speak.

"I know, I know," Torres said. "Just heard today. They're folding it into Saint Cecilia's. Believe that?" He shook his head. "The guys with the guns sound like anyone ever came in here before?"

Bob was still back on Saint Dom's. Torres, he suspected, liked to fuck with a man.

"They sounded like a thousand guys who've been in here before."

"And what do those thousand guys sound like?"

Bob gave it some thought. "Like they're just getting over a cold."

Torres smiled again, but this time it seemed genuine. "That sounds about right for this part of town."

OUT BACK A COUPLE minutes later, Rardy sat on a gurney behind the ambulance as the two patrolwomen left in their unit, and one of the EMTs tried to get a tall can of Narragansett out of Rardy's hand.

"You have a concussion," the guy said.

Rardy snatched the beer back. "The beer didn't cause it."

The EMT looked at Cousin Marv, who took the beer out of Rardy's hand. "It's for the best."

Rardy reached for the beer and called Marv a douche bag.

Torres and Bob were watching the miniconflict when Torres said, "Whole thing's a travesty."

"He'll be okay," Bob said.

Torres looked at him. "I meant Saint Dom's. Beautiful church. And they did mass right. No group hug after the Our Father, no folk singers." He looked down the alley with a hopeless victim's gaze. "Time the seculars get done persecuting the Church, all we'll have left is a bunch of condos with stained glass windows."

Bob said, "But . . ."

Torres gave him the righteous glare of a martyr watching pagans build his bonfire. "But what?"

"Well . . ." Bob spread his hands.

"No, what?"

"If the Church'd come clean—"

Torres squared himself, nothing playful in his eyes anymore. "That was it, uh? You don't see the *Globe* doing front-page articles on abuse cases in the Muslim world."

Bob knew he should shut his fucking mouth, but something took hold of him. "They covered up child rape. Under Rome's instruction."

"They said *sorry*."

"Was it meaningful, though?" Bob asked. "If they don't release the names of the priests who raped—"

Torres threw his hands at the air. "Cafeteria Catholicism did this. People wanting to be mostly Catholic, except for, you know, the hard parts. Why don't you take Communion?"

"*What?*"

"I've seen you at mass for years. You haven't taken Communion once."

Bob felt bewildered and violated. "That's my business."

Torres finally smiled again, but it was a smile so vicious Bob could have smelled it with his eyes closed.

Torres said, "You think so, uh?" and walked to his car.

Bob crossed to the ambulance, wondering what the fuck had just happened. But he knew what had happened—he'd made an enemy of a cop. A life spent living in a cubbyhole of airtight anonymity and the cubbyhole just got dumped all over the street.

The EMTs prepared to lift Rardy's gurney into the ambulance.

Bob said, "Moira meeting you?"

Rardy said, "I called her, yeah." He swiped the beer can out of Marv's hand and drained it. "Fucking hurts like a bastard, my head. Like a bastard."

They lifted him into the ambulance. Bob caught the empty beer can when he tossed it, and the EMTs shut the back doors and drove away.

Marv and Bob stood in the sudden quiet.

"The cop let you wear his letter jacket, or you have to let him give your nips a twist first?"

Bob sighed.

Marv wouldn't let it go. "Fuck you tell him about the watch for?"

"I don't know," Bob said and it dawned on him that he didn't. He had no idea.

Marv said, "Well, let's nip that fucking impulse in the bud for the rest of, you know, your life." He lit a cigarette and stamped his feet in the cold. "We got hit for five thou' and change. But Anwar and Makkhal picked up our envelope, so I'm not on the hook for that."

"So we're okay."

"We got clipped for five large," Marv said. "It's their bar, their money. We're not too fucking okay."

They looked back up the alley. They both shivered in the cold. After a while, they went back inside.

CHAPTER 4

Second City

On Sunday morning, Nadia brought the puppy to his car as he idled in front of her house. She handed it through the window and gave them both a little wave.

He looked at the puppy sitting on his seat and fear washed over him. What does it eat? When does it eat? Housebreaking. How do you do that? How long does it take? He'd had days to consider these questions—why were they only occurring to him now?

He hit the brakes and reversed the car a few feet. Nadia, one foot on her bottom step, turned back. He rolled down the passenger window, craned his body across the seat until he was looking up at her.

"I don't know what to do," he said. "I don't know anything."

AT A SUPERMARKET FOR pets, Nadia picked out several chew toys, told Bob he'd need them if he wanted to keep his couch. Shoes, she told him, keep your shoes hidden from now on, up on a high shelf. They bought vitamins—for a dog!—and a bag of puppy food she recommended, telling him the most important thing was to stick with that brand from now on. Change a dog's diet, she warned, you'll get piles of diarrhea on your floor.

They got the crate to put him in when Bob was at work. They got a water bottle for the crate and a book on dog training written by monks who were on the cover looking hardy and not real monkish, big smiles. As the cashier rang it all up, Bob felt a quake rumble through his body, a momentary disruption as he reached for his wallet. His throat flushed with heat. His head felt fizzy. And only as the quake went away and his throat cooled and his head cleared and he handed over his credit card to the cashier did he realize in the sudden disappearance of the feeling what the feeling was:

For a moment—maybe even a succession of moments and none sharp enough to point to as the cause—he'd been happy.

"SO, THANK YOU," SHE said when he pulled up in front of her house.

"What? No. Thank you. Please. Really. It . . . Thank you."

She said, "This little guy, he's a good guy. He's going to make you proud, Bob."

Bob looked down at the puppy, sleeping on her lap now, snoring slightly. "Do they do that? Sleep all the time?"

"Pretty much. Then they run around like loonies for about twenty minutes. Then they sleep some more. And poop. Bob, man, you got to remember that—they poop and pee like crazy. Don't get mad. They don't know any better. Read the books. It takes time, but they figure out soon enough not to do it in the house."

"What's soon enough?"

"Two months?" She cocked her head. "Maybe three. Be patient, Bob."

"Be patient," he repeated.

"And you too," she said to the puppy as she lifted it off her lap. He came awake, sniffing, snorting. He didn't want her to go. "You two take care," she said and let herself out, gave Bob a wave as she walked up her steps and then went inside.

The puppy was on its haunches, looking up at the window like Nadia might reappear there. He looked back over his shoulder at Bob. Bob could feel his abandonment. He could feel his own. He was certain they'd make a mess of it, him and this throwaway dog. He was sure the world was too strong.

"What's your name?" he asked the puppy. "What are we going to call you?"

The puppy turned his head away like, Bring the girl back.

FIRST THING IT DID was take a shit in the dining room.

Bob didn't even realize what it was doing at first. It started sniffing, nose scraping the rug, and then it looked up at Bob with an air of embarrassment. And Bob said, "What?" and the dog dumped all over the corner of the rug.

Bob scrambled forward, as if he could stop it, push it back in, and the puppy bolted, left droplets on the hardwood as it scurried into the kitchen.

Bob said, "No, no. It's okay." Although it wasn't. Most everything in the house had been his mother's, largely unchanged since she'd purchased it in the 1950s. That was shit. Excrement. In his mother's house. On her rug, her floor.

In the seconds it took him to reach the kitchen, the puppy'd left a piss puddle on the linoleum. Bob almost slipped in it. The puppy was sitting against the fridge, looking at him, tensing for a blow, trying not to shake.

And it stopped Bob. It stopped him, even as he knew the longer he left the shit on the rug the harder it would be to get out.

Bob got down on all fours. He felt the sudden return of what he'd felt when he first picked the dog out of the trash, something he'd assumed had left with Nadia. Connection.

He suspected they might have been brought together by something other than chance.

He said, "Hey." Barely above a whisper. "Hey, it's all right." So, so slowly, he extended his hand, and the puppy pressed itself harder against the fridge. But Bob kept the hand coming, and gently laid his palm on the side of the animal's face. He made soothing sounds. He smiled at it. He said "It's okay" over and over.

THESE DAYS DETECTIVE EVANDRO Torres worked Robbery Division, but before that, he'd been somebody. For one glorious year plus three months, he'd been a Homicide detective. Then, as he usually did with the good things in his life, he fucked it all up and got bounced down to Robbery.

At end of shift, Robbery did its drinking at JJ's, Homicide at The Last Drop, but if you wanted to find someone from Major Crimes, they were usually upholding the time-honored tradition of drinking in their cars down by the Pen' Channel.

That's where Torres found Lisa Romsey and her partner, Eddie Dexter. Eddie was a thin, sallow man who had no friends or family anyone knew of. He had the personality of a wet sandbox, and he never spoke unless spoken to, but he was an encyclopedia when it came to the New England mob.

Lisa Romsey was something else entirely—the hottest, prickliest Latina who'd ever strapped on a gun. The name

Romsey was the leftover of her two-year disaster of a marriage to the DA, and she kept it because, in this city, it still opened more doors than it shut. She'd partnered with Torres a few years back on a task force. After that disbanded, she got sent to Major Crimes, where she stayed, and Torres reached Homicide, where he didn't.

Evandro found them both sitting in their unmarked in the southern corner of the parking lot, drinking from cardboard Dunkin' Donuts cups with no steam coming out of them. Their unit faced the channel, so Evandro pulled his car into the next slot, pointing in the opposite direction, and rolled down his window.

Romsey rolled hers down after giving him a look that said she was debating leaving it up.

"What's the sunset nightcap this evening?" Torres asked. "Scotch or vodka?"

"Vodka," Romsey said. "You bring your own cup?"

"I just come out of the womb?" Torres handed her a ceramic coffee cup that had WORLD'S #1 DAD stenciled on it. Romsey arched an eyebrow at the words but poured vodka into the cup and handed it back.

They all took a drink, Eddie Dexter staring hard out the windshield like he was trying to find the sun in a sky so gray it could have been the wall to a prison.

Romsey said, "So what up, Evandro?"

"You remember Marvin Stipler from the day?"

Romsey shook her head.

"Cousin Marv?" Torres said. "He got pushed off his own book—what was it?—nine, ten years ago by the Chechens."

Romsey was nodding now. "Right, right, right. They came in, told him he had little Tic Tac testes. He spent the next decade proving them right."

Torres said, "That's the guy. His bar got held up the other night. Bar's owned by one of Papa Umarov's shell companies."

Romsey and Eddie Dexter exchanged surprised looks and then Romsey said, "Kinda retard holds up that kinda bar?"

"You got me. Major Crimes up on the Umarovs?"

Romsey poured herself another round and shook her head. "We barely survived the last budget cuts, we're not sticking our heads up to go after some Russian that John Q barely knows exists."

"Chechen."

"What?"

"They're Chechen, not Russian."

"Blow me."

Torres pointed at his wedding ring.

Romsey grimaced. "Oh, like that ever mattered."

"So Cousin Marv's not a dog anyone's got a stake in?"

Romsey shook her head. "You want him, Evandro, he's all yours."

"Thanks. Good to see you again, Lisa. You look great."

She batted her eyelashes at him, flipped him the bird, and rolled her window back up.

THE CITY WOKE THE next morning to four inches of snow. A month into winter and already they'd had three significant snowstorms and several dustings. If it kept this pace, come February there'd be no place to put it.

Bob and Cousin Marv each took a shovel out to the front of the bar, though Marv mostly leaned on his and wrapped his excuses in an old knee injury that nobody but Marv could recall.

Bob told him about his day with the dog and the cost of all the pet supplies and how the dog had taken a dump in the dining room.

Marv said, "You get the spot out of the rug?"

"I came close," Bob said. "But it's a dark rug."

Marv stared over the top of the shovel handle at him. "It's a dark . . . It's your mother's rug. I stepped on the thing with my shoe once—wasn't even dirty—and you tried to cut my foot off."

Bob said, "Listen to the drama queen," and it surprised both himself and Marv. Bob wasn't the type to give someone shit, particularly if that someone was Marv. But he had to admit, it felt good.

Marv recovered enough to grab his crotch and make a loud kissing noise and then he pushed his shovel through some snow for a minute, not doing much but lifting it off the asphalt enough for the breeze to catch it, fuck things up even more.

Two black Cadillac Escalades and a white van pulled up

to the curb, the rest of the street empty this time of day, and Bob didn't even have to look to know who'd be coming down here late on a snowy morning with two SUVs that were freshly washed and waxed.

Chovka Umarov.

"Cities," Bob's father once told him, "aren't run from the capitol building. They're run from the cellar. The First City? The one you see? That's the clothes they put over the body to make it look better. But the Second City *is* the body. That's where they take the bets and sell the women and the dope and the kinda TVs and couches and things a working man can afford. Only time a working man hears from the First City is when it's fucking him over. But the Second City is all around him every day his whole life."

Chovka Umarov was the Prince of the Second City.

Chovka's father, Papa Pytor Umarov, ran things these days, sharing power with the old Italian and Irish factions, working out subcontractor deals with the blacks and the Puerto Ricans, but it was accepted as stone cold truth in the streets that if Papa Pytor decided to be impolite and force any or all of his associates under his heel there wasn't a fucking thing they could do to stop him.

Anwar got out of the driver's seat of the lead SUV, eyes as cold as gin as he scowled at the weather like Bob and Marv were the cause of it.

Chovka exited the backseat of the same Escalade, pulling his gloves on and checking the ground for ice. Chovka's hair and trim beard were the same black as the gloves. He wasn't tall or short, wasn't big or small, but even with his back turned, he radiated an energy that made something itch in the base of Bob's skull. *The closer you get to Caesar,* one of Bob's high school history teachers had been fond of saying, *the greater the fear.*

Chovka stopped on the sidewalk by Bob and Marv, stood on a patch that Bob had already shoveled.

Chovka said to the street, "Who needs a snowblower when you got Bob?" And then to Bob, "Maybe you come to my house later."

Bob said, "Uh, sure," because he couldn't think of anything else to say.

The white van moved slightly from side to side. Bob was sure of it. The side closest to the curb dipped, and whatever weight caused the dip resettled in the middle and the van resettled with it.

Chovka chucked Bob's shoulder. "I'm kidding. This guy." He smiled at Anwar, then at Bob, but when he looked at Marv, his small black eyes got smaller and blacker still. "You on the welfare?"

A muffled thud emanated from the van. Could have been anything. The van rocked in place again.

"What?" Marv asked.

"What?" Chovka leaned back to get a better look at Marv.

"I meant, sorry."

"What're you sorry for?"

"I didn't understand your question."

"I asked if you on the welfare."

"No, no."

"No I didn't ask you?"

"No, I'm not on welfare."

Chovka pointed at the sidewalk and then their shovels. "Bob does all the work. You watch."

"No." Marv shoveled some snow, chucked it to his right into the pile. "I'm shoveling."

"You shoveling all right." Chovka lit a cigarette. "Come here."

Marv put a hand to his own chest, the question in his eyes.

"Both of you," Chovka said.

He led them down the sidewalk, the ice melt and rock salt crunching under their feet like broken glass. They stepped off the curb behind the van and Bob saw what could have been transmission fluid leaking out of the underside of the van. Except it was in the wrong place for tranny fluid. And it was the wrong color and consistency.

Chovka opened both van doors at once.

Two Chechens built like Dumpsters with feet sat on either side of a sweaty, thin guy. The thin guy was dressed like a construction worker—blue plaid shirt over a thermal and tan denim pants. They'd gagged his mouth with a cotton scarf and drilled a six-inch metal bolt through the top of his right foot, which was bare, the boot tipped over just to the right of it, the sock sticking out of the boot. The guy's head drooped, but one of the Chechens pulled back on his hair and shoved a small amber vial under his nose. The guy got a good whiff and his head snapped back, his eyes snapped open, and he was wide awake again while the other Chechen used a chuck key to tighten the bit in a power drill.

"You know this guy?" Chovka asked.

Bob shook his head.

Marv said, "No."

Chovka said, "But *I* know this guy. Moment I know him? I know him. I try to explain to him when he come to me to do some business that he must have a moral center. Eh, Bob? You understand?"

"A moral center," Bob said. "Sure, Mr. Umarov."

"A man who has a moral center knows what he knows and knows what has to be done. He knows how to keep his affairs in order. A man with no moral center, however, does not know what he does not know and you can never explain it to him. Because if he knew the thing he did not know then he would have a moral center." He looked at Marv. "You understand?"

"I do," Marv said. "Absolutely."

Chovka grimaced. He smoked for a bit.

In the van, the construction worker whimpered and the Chechen on his left slapped the back of his head until he stopped.

"Somebody robbed my bar?" Chovka said to Bob.

"Yes, Mr. Umarov."

Chovka said, "You call my father 'Mister Umarov,' Bob. Me you call Chovka, hey?"

"Chovka. Yes, sir."

"Who robbed our bar?"

"We don't know," Cousin Marv said. "They wore masks."

Chovka said, "The police report said one wore a broken watch? You tell the police this?"

Marv looked down at his shovel.

Bob said, "I answered without thinking. I'm very sorry."

Chovka looked back at the construction worker for a bit and smoked and no one said anything.

Then Chovka asked Marv, "What have you done to get my father's money back?"

"We've got the word out in the neighborhood."

Chovka looked over at Anwar. "The word is out there. Like our money."

The guy in the van shit himself. They all heard it, and they all acted like they didn't.

Chovka closed the van doors. He knocked on the door with his fist twice and the van pulled away from the curb.

He turned to Bob and Marv. "Find our fucking money."

Chovka got back in the Escalade. Anwar paused at the door, looked at Bob, and pointed at a spot of snow Bob had missed. He followed his boss into the SUV, and both Escalades pulled away from the curb.

Cousin Marv saluted them as they reached the stop sign

and turned right. "And a Happy Fucking New Year to you as well, gents."

Bob shoveled for a bit in silence. Marv leaned on his shovel and watched the street.

"That guy in the van?" Marv said. "I don't ever want to talk about him or hear about him. We good on that?"

Bob didn't want to talk about him either. He nodded.

After a bit, Marv said, "How we supposed to find their money? If we knew where their money was that'd mean we knew who robbed us which would mean we were in on it which would mean they'd shoot us in the fucking face. So how we supposed to find their money?"

Bob kept shoveling because it was the kind of question there was no answer for.

Marv lit a Camel. "Fucking Chechneyans, man."

Bob stopped shoveling. "Chechens."

"What?"

"They're Chechens," Bob said, "not Chechneyans."

Marv didn't believe it. "But they're from Chechneya."

Bob shrugged. "Yeah, but you don't call people from Ireland 'Irelandians.'"

They leaned on their shovels and stared up the street for a while until Marv suggested they go back inside. It was cold, he said, and his knee was fucking killing him.

CHAPTER 5

Cousin Marv

IN LATE 1967, WHEN the good people of Boston elected Kevin White mayor, Cousin Marv's voice was deemed so beautiful he was plucked out of third grade to sing at the inauguration. Each morning, he attended Saint Dom's. But every afternoon, after lunch, he was bused across the city to train with a boys' choir at the Old South Church in Back Bay. The Old South Church sat at 645 Boylston Street—the rest of his life, Marv never forgot that address—and had been built in 1875. It sat diagonally across a plaza from Trinity Church, another architectural masterpiece, and within spitting distance of the Boston Public Library Main Branch and the Copley Plaza Hotel, four buildings so majestic that when little Marv was in them, even in their basements, he felt closer to the sky. Closer to Heaven, closer to God or any of the angels or other spirits that floated along the fringes of old paintings. Marv remembered having his first adult suspicion as a choirboy—that feeling closer to God had something to do with feeling closer to knowledge.

And then they kicked him out of the choir.

Another boy, Chad Benson—Marv would never forget that fucking name, either—claimed he saw Marv steal a Baby Ruth from Donald Samuel's schoolbag in the coat closet. Claimed it in front of the rest of the choir while the choirmaster and the instructors were all taking a piss break downstairs. Chad said they all knew Marv was poor but next time he wanted to eat just ask them and they'd give him charity. Marv told Chad Benson he was full of shit. Chad mocked Marv for sputtering and turning red. Then Chad called Marv a welfare case, asked if he'd got his clothes at the Bargain Basement in Quincy, and whether his whole family shopped there or just Marv and his mother. Marv punched Chad Benson in the face so hard the crack of it echoed through the sanctuary. When Chad hit the floor, Marv climbed on top of him, grabbed a hunk of his hair, and punched him twice more. It was the third punch that detached Chad's retina. Not that the injury, serious as it was, mattered in the grand scheme of things—Marv was done the moment he took his first swing at the prick. The Chad Bensons of the world, he learned that day, were never to be hit. They weren't even to be questioned. Not by the Marvin Stiplers of this life anyway.

In the process of kicking him out, Ted Bing, the choirmaster, delivered a further blow when he told Marv that according to his expert ear, Marv's voice would peak at the age of nine.

Marv was eight.

They didn't even let him take the bus home with the rest of the choir. Just gave him carfare, and he hopped the Red Line down under the city and back to East Buckingham. He waited until he was walking from the station back to his house before he ate Donald Samuel's Baby Ruth bar. It was the best meal, before or since, he'd ever tasted. It wasn't just the chocolate, slightly melted, but the rich buttery tang of self-pity that engaged every one of his taste buds and caressed his heart. To feel righteously enraged and tragically victimized at the same time was, Marv would very rarely admit to himself, better than any orgasm in the history of fucking.

Happiness made Marv anxious because he knew it didn't last. But happiness destroyed was worth wrapping your arms around because it always hugged you back.

His voice cracked at nine just as Ted Fucking Bing had said it would. No more singing in choirs for Marv. For the rest of his life Marv avoided downtown whenever possible. Those old buildings, once his gods, became heartless mirrors. He could see, reflected in them, all the versions of himself he'd never become.

After Chovka visited with his Gitmo-on-Wheels and his prick eyes and prick attitude, Marv had shoveled up the rest of the walk, bad knee and all, Bob just fucking watching the whole time, probably daydreaming about that dog he'd become so obsessed with you could barely talk to him anymore. They'd gone inside and, sure enough, Bob had started babbling about the dog again. Marv hadn't let on how boring it was because, truth be told, it was good to see Bob get excited about anything.

Bob's short stick in life wasn't just that he was raised by two old, homely parents with few friends and no connections. His true short stick was that those parents had babied him, smothered him so completely in a desperate love (connected, Marv suspected, to their own imminent passage from the land of the living), that Bob never learned how to fully survive in a man's world. Bob, it would surprise many who knew him now, could be pretty fearsome if you tripped the wrong switch in that slow brain of his, but there was another part of him that was so in need of a petting that it completely undercut the part of him that could fuck a person up if he were pushed hard enough against a wall.

Now he had the Chechen mob looking at them because he'd been stupid enough to give free information to a cop. And not just any cop, it turned out. A cop he *knew*. From church.

The Chechen mob. Looking at them. Because Bob was weak.

Marv got home early that night. Not much going on at the bar, no reason to stick around when he was paying Bob to do, you know, his fucking job. He paused in his mudroom to take off his coat and gloves and hat and scarf, winter being just one big fucking excuse to wear more shit than someone in Hawaii knew existed.

Dottie called from the kitchen. "That you?"

"Who's it gonna be?" he called back even though he'd promised himself he'd be kinder to his sister in the new year.

"Could be one of them kids claims to sell magazine subscriptions because he's working his way out of the ghetto."

He searched for a hook for his hat. "Wouldn't that kid ring the front doorbell?"

"They could slice your throat."

"Who?"

"Those kids."

"With magazines. What, they grab one of those, what do they call 'em, inserts, and bleed you out with a paper cut?"

"Your Steak-umm's on."

He could hear it sizzle. "On my way."

He kicked off his right boot with his left but then had to remove the left by hand. At the tip, it was dark. At first he thought it was the snow.

But no, it was blood.

Same blood had leaked out of that guy's foot, through the hole in the floor of the van, and onto the street.

Found Marv's boot.

Those Chechens, man. Those fucking Chechens.

Give a dumb man pause. Give a smart man ambition.

When he came into the kitchen, Dottie, in her housedress and fuzzy moose slippers, eyes on the pan, said, "You look tired."

"You didn't even look."

"I looked yesterday." She gave him a weary smile. "Now I'm looking."

Marv grabbed a beer from the fridge, trying to shake the image of that guy's foot from his head, of that sick fucking Chechen beside him tightening the drill with his chuck key.

"And?" he asked Dottie.

"You look tired," she said brightly.

AFTER DINNER, DOTTIE WENT into the den to catch up on her shows and Marv went to the gym on Dunboy. He'd already had a beer too many to work out but he could always catch a steam.

This time of night, there was no one in the steam room—there was barely anyone in the gym—and when Marv came out he felt so much better. It was almost like he had worked out, which, come to think of it, was usually what happened when he went to the gym.

He showered, part of him wishing he'd smuggled a beer in with him because there was nothing quite like a cold beer in a hot shower after a workout. When he came out, he dressed by his locker. Ed Fitzgerald stood at the next locker over and idly fiddled with the lock.

"I hear they're pissed," Fitz said.

Marv stepped into his cords. "They're not supposed to like it. They got robbed."

"Scary-fucking-Chechen pissed." Fitz sniffled and Marv was pretty sure it wasn't from the cold.

"No, they're fine. You're fine. Just keep your head down. Your brother too." He looked at Fitz as he laced up his shoes. "What's up with his watch?"

"Why?"

"I noticed it doesn't work."

Fitz looked embarrassed. "It never did. Our old man gave it to him for his tenth birthday. It stopped, like, the next day. Old man couldn't return it because he'd stole it in the first place. He'd tell Bri, 'Don't bitch—it's right twice a day.' Bri don't go anywhere without it."

Marv buttoned his shirt up over his wife-beater. "Well, he should get a new one."

"When we going to hit a place that's holding the actual drop? I don't like risking my life, my fucking freedom, my, ya know, everything for five fucking grand."

Marv closed his locker, his coat over his arm. "Let's just assume I'm not an asshole without a plan. When an airplane crashes, what's the safest airline to fly the next day?"

"The one that had the crash."

Marv gave him a big shit-eating grin. "There you go."

Fitz followed him out of the locker room. "I don't understand a word you're saying. It's like you're speaking Brazilian."

"Brazilians speak Portuguese."

"Yeah?" Fitz said. "Well, fuck them."

CHAPTER 6

Via Crucis

AFTER EVERYONE HAD FILED out of the seven o'clock mass, including Detective Torres, who shot Bob a look of flat contempt as he passed, and Father Regan had retired to the sacristy to change out of his vestments and wash the chalices (a job once left to the altar boys, but you couldn't find altar boys to do the seven anymore), Bob remained in his pew. He didn't pray exactly, but he did sit in the embrace of a silent hush rarely found outside of a church to reflect on an eventful week. Bob could remember whole years in which nothing had happened to him. Years when he'd look up expecting the calendar to read March and see November instead. But in the past seven days, he'd found the dog (as yet unnamed), met

Nadia, been robbed at gunpoint, adopted the dog, and been visited by a gangster who tortured men in the back of a van.

He looked up at the vaulted ceiling. He looked out at the marble altar. He looked over at the stations of the cross, each placed evenly between the stained glass saints. The Way of Sorrows, each station a sculpture depicting Christ's final journey in the temporal world, from condemnation through crucifixion to entombment. There were fourteen stations spaced throughout the church. Bob could have drawn them from memory if he'd been any good at drawing. Same could be said of the stained glass saints, starting with Saint Dominic, of course, patron saint of hopeful mothers, but not to be confused with the other Saint Dominic, patron saint of the falsely accused and founder of the Dominican Order. Most members of Saint Dominic's parish didn't know there were two Saint Dominics and, if they did, had no idea which of them their church was named after. But Bob did. His father, head usher for this church for many years and the most devout man Bob had ever met, had known, of course, and had passed down the knowledge to his son.

You didn't tell me, Dad, that the world contained men who beat dogs and left them to die in frigid trash cans or men who drilled bolts through the feet of other men.

I didn't have to tell you. Cruelty is older than the Bible. Savagery beat its chest in the first human summer and has kept beating it every day since. The worst in men is commonplace. The best is a far rarer thing.

Bob walked the stations. Via Crucis. He paused at the fourth, where Jesus met His mother as He carried the cross up the hill, the crown of thorns on His head, two centurions standing behind Him with their whips, ready to use them, to drive Him from His mother, to force Him up the hill, where they would nail Him to the very cross they forced Him to drag. Had those centurions repented later in life? Could there *be* repentance?

Or were some sins simply too big?

The Church said no. As long as there was meaningful penance, the Church said God would forgive. But the Church was an interpretive vessel, at times an imperfect one. So what if, in this case, the Church was wrong? What if some souls could never be reclaimed from the black pits of their sin?

If Heaven was to be considered a valued destination, then Hell must hold twice as many souls.

Bob hadn't even realized he'd lowered his head until he raised it.

To the left of the fourth station of the cross was Saint Agatha, patron saint of nurses and bakers, among other things, and to the right was Saint Rocco, patron saint of bachelors, pilgrims, and . . .

Bob stepped back in the aisle to get a better look at a stained glass window he'd passed so many times he'd long since lost his ability to see it. And there in the lower right-hand corner of the window, looking up at his saint and master, was a dog.

Rocco, patron saint of bachelors, pilgrims, and . . . Dogs.

"ROCCO," NADIA SAID WHEN he told her. "I . . . like it. That's a good name."

"You think? I almost named him Cassius."

"Why?"

"Because I thought he was a boxer."

"And?"

"Cassius Clay," he explained.

"Was he a boxer?"

"Yeah. Changed his name to Muhammad Ali."

"Him, I heard of," she said and Bob suddenly didn't feel so old. But then she said, "Doesn't he have a grill named after him?"

"No, that's the other guy."

Bob, Nadia, and the newly minted Rocco walked along a path by the river in Pen' Park. Nadia came around after work sometimes, and she and Bob took Rocco out. Bob knew something was a little off about Nadia—the dog being found so close to her house and her lack of surprise or interest in that fact was not lost on Bob—but was there anyone, anywhere on this planet, who wasn't a little off? More than a little most times. Nadia came by to help with the dog, and Bob, who hadn't known much friendship in his life, took what he could get.

They taught Rocco to sit and lie down and paw and roll over. Bob read the entire monk book and followed its instructions. The puppy was dewormed and cured of kennel cough by the vet before it really got a chance to start. He had his rabies shot, his parvo booster, and had been cleared of any serious damage to his head. Just deep bruises, the vet said, just deep bruises. He was registered. He grew fast.

Now Nadia was teaching them both how to "heel."

"Okay, Bob, now stop hard and say it."

Bob stopped and pulled up on the leash to get Rocco to sit by his left foot. Rocco half-swung with the leash. Then he twirled. Then he lay on his back.

"Heel. No, Rocco. Heel."

Rocco sat up. He stared at Bob.

"Okay," Nadia said. "Not bad, not bad. Walk ten steps, do it again."

Bob and Rocco walked down the path. Bob stopped. "Heel."

Rocco sat.

"Good boy." Bob gave him a treat.

They walked another ten steps, tried it again. This time Rocco jumped as high as Bob's hip, landed on his side, and rolled over several times.

"Heel," Bob said. "Heel."

They walked another ten steps and it worked.

Tried it again. And failed.

Bob looked at Nadia. "It takes time, right?"

Nadia nodded. "Some more than others. You two? I think it'll take a while."

A bit later, Bob let Rocco off leash, and the puppy bolted off the path into the trees, raced back and forth among the trunks closest to the path.

"He won't go far from you," Nadia said. "You notice? He keeps his eye on you."

Bob flushed with pride. "He sleeps on my leg when I watch TV."

"Yeah?" Nadia smiled. "He still having accidents in the house?"

Bob sighed. "Oh, yeah."

About a hundred yards deeper in the park, they stopped by the restrooms and Nadia went in the ladies' while Bob put Rocco back on leash and gave him another treat.

"Nice-looking dog."

Bob turned, saw a young guy passing them. Lanky hair, lanky build, pale eyes, small silver hoop in his left earlobe.

Bob gave the guy a nod and a smile of thanks.

The guy stood on the path, several feet away and said, "That's a nice-looking dog."

Bob said, "Thanks."

"A *handsome* dog."

Bob looked over at the guy, but he'd already turned and was walking away. He flipped a hood off his shoulders and over his head and walked with his hands in his pockets and his shoulders hunched against the raw weather.

Nadia exited the ladies' room and saw something in Bob's face.

"What's up?"

Bob chin-gestured up the path. "That guy kept saying Rocco was a nice-looking dog."

Nadia said, "Rocco is a nice-looking dog."

"Yeah, but . . ."

"But what?"

Bob shrugged and let it pass, even though he knew there was more to it. He could feel it—something in the fabric of the world had just torn.

THESE DAYS, MARV HAD to pay for it.

After his half hour with Fantasia Ibanez, he left and headed home. He met Fantasia once a week in the room at the back of the whorehouse Betsy Cannon ran out of one of the old wardens' mansions on the top of the crest in The Heights. The houses up there were all Second Empire Victorians and had been built back in the 1800s when the prison had been the main source of work in East Buckingham. The prison was long gone; all that remained of it were the names—Pen' Park, Justice Lane, Probation Avenue, and the oldest bar in the neighborhood, The Gallows.

Marv walked down the hill into the Flats, surprised at how warm it had gotten today, up in the forties and holding into the evening, the gutters all gurgling with streams of melted snow, the drainpipes voiding gray liquid onto the side-walks, the wood frame homes sporting pimples of moisture, like they'd spent the afternoon sweating.

Nearing the house, he wondered how he'd become a guy who lived with his sister and paid for sex. This afternoon, he'd gone to visit the old man, Marv Sr., and he'd told him a bunch of lies even though the old man had no idea he was even in the room. He told his father he'd taken advantage of the hot mar-ket in commercial real estate and the limited supply of liquor licenses in this city and he'd cashed in, sold Cousin Marv's Bar for a mint. Enough to get his father in a real good home, that German one over in West Roxbury, maybe, if he greased the right palms. And now he could. Once all the paperwork was signed and the money released by the bank—"You know banks, Pop, they'll hold on to it until you resort to begging for your own money"—Marv could take care of the family again, just like he had in his heyday.

Except the old man hadn't accepted his money back then. The old man was fucking annoying that way, asking Marv in his broken Polack (Stipler was an Americanization, and not a very good one, of Stepanski) why he couldn't work an honest job like his father, mother, and sister.

Marvin Sr. had been a cobbler, his wife worked in a Laun-dromat for thirty years, and Dottie pushed paper for Allstate. Marv would sooner sell his dick to science than work a coolie career for coolie wages the rest of his life. Wake up at the end of it all and ask, What the fuck happened?

Yet for all their conflict, he loved the old man and, he liked to hope, vice versa. They caught a lot of Sox games together and held their own in the 50 Tenpin Bowling League once a week, the old man a deadeye for picking up the 7–10 split. Then came the stroke, followed a year later by the heart attack, followed three months after that by the second stroke. Now Marvin Stipler Senior sat in a dim room that smelled of mold, and not the kind of mold you found in wet walls but the kind you found in people as they neared the end. Still, Marv held out hope that the old man was in there somewhere and he was coming back. And not just coming back but coming back with a glint in his eyes. Lots of stranger things had happened in this world. Trick was to not give up hope. Not give up hope and go get some money, put him in a place where they believed in miracles, not warehousing.

In the house, he grabbed a beer, a shot of Stoli, and his ashtray and joined Dottie in the small den where they had the TV and the Barcaloungers set up. Dottie was working her way through a bowl of Rocky Road. She claimed it was her second, so Marv knew it was her third, but who was he to begrudge the things that gave a person pleasure? He lit a cigarette and stared at a commercial for motorized floor sweepers, the little fuckers buzzing around some toothy housewife's floors like things that turned against you in sci-fi movies. Marv figured pretty soon that toothy housewife would open a closet, find a couple of the little robot saucers whispering their conspiracy to each other. And then she'd be the first to go, each of the little fuckers taking an end and just sucking her to pieces.

Marv had a lot of ideas like this. One of these days, he kept telling himself, he needed to write them down.

When *American Idol* returned, Dottie turned in her recliner and said, "We should join that show."

"You can't sing," he reminded her.

She waved her spoon. "No, the other one—people going around the world looking for the clues and stuff."

"*The Amazing Race?*"

She nodded.

Marv patted her arm. "Dottie, you're my sister and I love you, but between my smokes and your ice cream, they're, what, gonna run beside us with defibrillators and those fucking shock paddles? Every ten steps we take—*Bzzt! Bzzt!*"

Dottie's spoon scraped the bottom of her bowl. "It'd be fun. We'd see things."

"What things?"

"Other countries, other ways."

It hit Marv—when they did jack the drop bar, he'd *have to* leave the country. No way out of that one. Jesus. Say good-bye to Dottie? Not even say good-bye. Just go. Man, oh man, the world asked a lot of ambitious men.

"You see Dad today?"

"I was by."

"They want their money, Marv."

Marv looked around the room. "Who?"

"The home," Dottie said.

"They'll get it." Marv stubbed out his cigarette, exhausted suddenly. "They'll get it."

Dottie put her bowl on the TV dinner table between them. "It's collection agencies calling now, not the home. You know? Medicare cuts, me retiring . . . They'll ship him off."

"To where?"

"A lesser place."

"There is one?"

She looked at him carefully. "Maybe it's time."

Marv lit a cigarette, even though his throat was still raw meat from the last one. "Just kill him, you're saying. Our father. He's inconvenient."

"He's dead, Marv."

"Yeah? What're those beeps coming out of the machines? Those waves on the screen of the thing? That's life."

"That's electricity."

Marv closed his eyes. The darkness was warm, inviting. "I put his hand to my face today?" He opened his eyes, looked at his sister. "I could hear his blood."

Neither of them spoke for so long that *American Idol* had moved on to a new set of commercials by the time Dottie cleared her throat and opened her mouth.

"I'll get to Europe in another life," she said.

Marv met her eyes and nodded his thanks.

After a minute, he patted her leg. "You want some more Rocky Road?"

She handed the bowl to him.

CHAPTER 7

Deeds

WHEN EVANDRO TORRES WAS five years old, he got stuck on the Ferris wheel at Paragon Park in Nantasket Beach. His parents had let him go on the ride alone. To this day he couldn't understand the fuck they'd been thinking or fully comprehend that the park personnel had let a five-year-old sit alone in a seat that went a hundred feet in the air. But back then, shit, child safety wasn't a big concern to most people; you asked your old man for a seat belt while he was barreling along 95 with a Schlitz tall between his legs, he handed you his tie, told you to figure it out.

So there was little Evandro, sitting at the meridian of the wheel's rotation when it jammed, sitting under a white sun that beat on his face and head like a bee swarm, and if he looked to his left he could see the park and then the rest of Hull and Weymouth beyond. He could even make out parts of Quincy. To his right though was ocean—ocean and more ocean and then the Harbor Islands followed by the Boston skyline. And he realized he was seeing things as God saw things.

It chilled him to realize how small and breakable everything was—every building, every person.

When they finally got the wheel going again and got him down, they thought he was crying because the height had scared him. And truth was he'd never be a real fan of heights ever again, but that wasn't why he wept. He wept— and did so for so long that while they were riding home, his father, Hector, threatened to throw him out of the car without coming off the gas—because he understood that life was finite. Yeah, yeah, he'd tell the one shrink he went to after his second demotion, I get it—we all understand life ends. But actually, we don't. Somewhere in the back of our heads, we think we're going to beat it. We think something's going to happen to change the deal—a new scientific discovery, the Second Coming, ETs, *something*—and we'll live forever. But at five—at fucking *five*—he'd known with crystalline clarity that he, Evandro Manolo Torres, was going to die. Maybe not today. But, then again, maybe so.

This knowledge placed a ticking clock in the center of his head and a bell in his heart that tolled on the hour, every hour.

And so Evandro prayed. And he went to mass. And he read his Bible. And he tried to commune every day with the Lord Our Savior and Heavenly Father.

And he drank too much.

And, for a while there, he also smoked too much and chipped cocaine, both nasty habits, but both now more than five years in his rearview.

And he loved his wife and his kids and he tried to make sure they knew it and felt it every day.

But it wasn't enough. The gap—the fucking chasm, the hole, the abscess at the center of him—would not close. Whatever else the world saw when they looked at him, when Evandro looked at himself, he saw a man running toward a point on the horizon he could never reach. And one day in the middle of the running the lights would simply go out. Never to be turned on again. Not in this world.

And it made the clock tick faster and the bell toll louder, made Evandro Torres feel crazed and helpless and needing something—anything—to anchor him in the now.

That something, since he was old enough to know about it, was flesh.

Which is how he found himself in Lisa Romsey's bed for the first time in two years, the two of them going at it like they hadn't missed a beat, finding their rhythm before they even landed on the mattress, their breath and skin smelling of alcohol, but it was hot breath, hot skin. And when he came, Evandro felt it even in the smallest bones in his body. Lisa came at the same time, the moan that escaped her throat so loud it lifted the ceiling.

It took about four seconds for him to get off her and five more for the regret to set in.

She sat up on the bed and reached across him for the bottle of red on the nightstand. She drank from the bottle. She said, "Jesus." She said, "Man." She said, "Shit."

She handed the bottle to Torres.

He took a drink. "Hey, it happens."

"Don't mean it should, you asshole."

"Why am I the asshole?"

"Because you're married."

"Not well."

She took the bottle back. "You mean not happily."

"No," Torres said, "I mean, we're happy mostly, but we just don't do the whole domestic-faithful thing well. It's like fucking string theory to us. Man, I got to look my priest in the eye tomorrow and confess this shit."

Romsey said, "You're the worst Catholic I've ever heard of."

Torres widened his eyes at that and chuckled. "I'm not even close."

"How's that possible, Sinnerman?"

"The point isn't not sinning," he explained. "The point is accepting that you're born fallen and life is trying to atone for that."

Romsey rolled her eyes. "Why don't you fall your ass out of my bed then and get gone?"

Torres sighed and climbed out from under the sheets. He sat on the edge of the bed and put on his pants, searched for his shirt and socks. He caught Romsey in the mirror watching him, and he knew that despite her best efforts, she liked him.

Thank you, Jesus, for the minor miracles.

Romsey lit a cigarette. "After you left the other day, I did a little surfing regards to your drop bar, Cousin Marv's."

Torres found one sock but not the other. "Yeah?"

"It got mentioned in an unsolved from a decade ago."

Torres stopped looking for the sock for a moment. He looked up the bed at her. "No shit?"

She reached behind her back, returned with something he couldn't quite make out. She flicked her wrist and his sock landed by his hip. "Kid named Richard Whelan walked out of there one night, no one ever saw him again. If you solved a ten-years-cold 187, Evandro?"

"I could make it back to Homicide."

She frowned. "You'll never make it back to Homicide."

"Why not?"

"Ne-ver."

"Why not?" he said again. He knew the answer but he was hoping it had somehow changed.

Her eyes bugged. "Because Scarpone runs it."

"And?"

"And you fucked his wife, you shithead. Then drove her home drunk on duty, and smashed up the fucking unit you were driving."

Torres closed his eyes. "Okay, so I'll never make it back to Homicide."

"But you solve this kind of cold case, you might make it to Major Crimes."

"Yeah?"

She smiled at him. "Yeah."

Torres put on his sock, liking that idea a lot.

I was lost, he'd say on the day of his transfer, *but now am found.*

MARV WALKED OUT OF Cottage Market with two coffees, a bag of pastries, the *Herald* under his arm, and ten Big Buckaroo scratch tickets from Mass Millions in his coat pocket.

A long time ago, in the proudest but hardest moment of his life, Marv had walked away from cocaine. He'd fallen into some money unexpectedly and he'd done the right thing— paid off his debts and cleaned the fuck up. *Until* that day, however, he'd been a fucking degenerate with no dignity and no control. But once he paid off that debt and walked away, he took his dignity back. Since then, he may have let his body go to the point that only pros would fuck him, and it was probably true he'd burned more relationships than most people had hair, but he had his dignity.

He also had ten scratch tickets that he'd parcel out to himself slowly tonight while Dottie watched *Survivor* or *Un-*

dercover Boss or whatever fucking "reality" show was teed up for the evening.

As he stepped off the curb, a car slowed in front of him. Then stopped.

The passenger window whirred as it descended.

The driver leaned across the seat and said, "Hey."

Marv glanced at the car, then the guy. Car was a 2011-or-so Jetta. Kind of car college kids or ones just out of college drove, but this guy was in his early forties. There was something memorably forgettable about him, a face so bland you couldn't place the features when they were swimming right in front of you. Marv got a whiff of earth tones off the guy—light brown hair, light brown eyes, tan clothes.

The guy said, "You tell me where the hospital is?"

Marv said, "You need to bang a U-ey, go back two–three miles. It's on the left."

"On the left?"

"Yeah."

"My left."

"Your left."

"Not yours."

"We're both facing the same direction."

"We are?"

"Generally speaking."

"Okay then." The guy smiled at him. It could have been a smile of thanks, but it could have been something else, something off-kilter and unknowable. Impossible to tell. His eyes still on Marv, he pinned the wheel and executed a perfect U-turn.

Marv watched him go and tried to ignore the sweat running down his thighs on a thirty-degree day.

BOB SHRUGGED INTO HIS coat, ready for another day at the bar. He went into the kitchen where Rocco was chewing the hell out of a rawhide stick. He filled Rocco's water bowl, looked around the kitchen until he spied the yellow duck chew toy Rocco carried everywhere. He laid it in the corner of the crate. He put the water bowl in the other corner. He snapped his fingers lightly.

Bob said, "Come on, boy. Crate."

Rocco trotted into the crate and curled up against the yellow duck. Bob petted his face, then closed the door.

"See you tonight." Bob passed down the hall to the front door and opened it.

The guy on the porch was thin. Not weak-thin. Hard-thin. As if whatever burned inside of him burned so hot that fat couldn't survive. His blue eyes were so pale they were almost gray. His lanky hair was as blond as the goatee that clung to his lips and chin. Bob recognized him immediately—the kid who'd passed him in the park the other day and said Rocco was a good-looking dog.

Upon closer inspection, no kid actually. Probably thirty when you got a close look.

He smiled and stuck out his hand. "Mr. Saginowski?"

Bob shook the hand. "Yes."

"Bob Saginowski?" The man shook Bob's large hand with his small one, and there was a lot of power in the grip.

"Yeah."

"Eric Deeds, Bob." The kid let go of his hand. "I believe you have my dog."

Bob felt like he'd been slapped across the face with a bag of ice. "What?"

Eric Deeds hugged himself. "Brrrr. Cold out here, Bob. Not fit for man nor . . . Where is he by the way?"

He made to go past Bob. Bob stepped in front of him. He sized Bob up, smiled.

"I bet he's back there. You keep him in the kitchen? Or down the cellar?"

Bob said, "What're you talking about?"

Eric said, "The dog."

Bob said, "Look, you liked my dog in the park the other day, but—"

Eric said, "He's not your dog."

Bob said, "What? He's mine."

Eric shook his head the way nuns did when they'd caught you dead in your lie. "You got a minute to talk?" He held his index finger up. "Just one minute."

IN THE KITCHEN, ERIC Deeds said, "Hey, there he is." He said, "That's my guy." He said, "He got big." He said, "The size of him."

When Bob opened the crate, it broke his heart to see Rocco slink over to Eric Deeds. He even climbed up on his lap when Eric, unbidden, took a seat at Bob's kitchen table and patted his inner thigh twice. Bob couldn't even say how it was the guy had talked his way into the house; he was just one of those people had a way about him, like cops and Teamsters—he wanted in, he was coming in.

"Bob," Eric Deeds said, "you know a chick name of Nadia Dunn?" He rubbed Rocco's belly. Bob felt a prick of envy as Rocco kicked his left leg, even though a constant shiver—almost a palsy—ran through his fur.

"Nadia Dunn?" Bob said.

"It's not a I-know-so-many-Nadias-I-get-'em-confused kinda name, man." Eric Deeds scratched under Rocco's chin. Rocco's ears and tail stayed pressed flat to his body. He looked ashamed, his eyes staring down into their own sockets.

"I know her." Bob reached out and lifted Rocco off Eric's lap, plopped him down on his own, scratched behind his ears. "She's helped me walk Rocco a few times."

The act was between them now, Bob lifting the puppy off Eric's lap without any warning, Eric looking at him for just a second, like, The fuck was *that* all about? Eric still had a smile on his face, but it wasn't big anymore, and it wasn't happy. His forehead narrowed, and it gave his eyes a surprised cast, as if they'd never expected to find themselves on his face. In that moment, he looked cruel, the kind of guy, if he was feeling sorry for himself, took a shit on the whole world.

"Rocco?" he said.

Bob nodded as Rocco's ears unfurled from his head and he licked Bob's wrist. "That's his name. What did you call him?"

"Called him Dog mostly. Sometimes Hound."

Eric Deeds looked around the kitchen, up at the old circular fluorescent in the ceiling, something going back to Bob's mother, hell, Bob's father around the time the old man had also been obsessed with paneling—paneled the kitchen, the living room, the dining room, would've paneled the toilet if he could've figured out how.

"Bob, I'm going to need my dog back."

For a second, Bob lost his ability to form words. "He's mine," he said eventually.

Eric shook his head. "You've been leasing him from me." He looked over at the dog in Bob's arms. "Lease is up."

"You beat him."

Eric reached into his shirt pocket. He pulled out a cigarette and popped it in his mouth. He lit it, shook out the match, and tossed it on Bob's kitchen table.

"You can't smoke in here."

Eric considered Bob with a level gaze and kept smoking. "I beat him?"

"Yeah."

"Uh, so what?" Eric flicked some ash on the floor. "I'm taking the dog, Bob."

Bob stood to his full height. He held tight to Rocco, who

squirmed a bit in his arms and nipped at the flat of his hand. If it came to it, Bob decided, he'd drop all six foot three inches and 250 pounds of himself on Eric Deeds, who couldn't weigh more than a buck-seventy. Not now, not just standing there, but if Eric reached for Rocco, well then . . .

Eric Deeds smiled up at him. "You're getting all yippee ki-yay on my shit, Bob? Sit down. Really." Eric leaned back in the chair and blew a stream of smoke at the ceiling. "I asked you if you knew Nadia because I know Nadia. She lives on my block, has since we were kids. It's the funny thing about a neighborhood, you might not know a lot of people, particularly if they're not your age, but you know *everyone* on your block." He looked over at Bob as Bob sat back down. "I saw you that night. I was feeling bad, you know, about my temper? So I went back to see if the hound was really dead or not and I watched you pluck him out of the trash and then go up to Nadia's porch. You all into her, Bob?"

Bob said, "I really think you should go."

"I wouldn't blame you. She's no beauty queen but she's not a schnauzer. And you're no pinup, are you, Bob?"

Bob pulled his cell from his pocket and flipped it open. "I'm calling 911."

"Be my guest." Eric nodded. "You register him, all that? City says you gotta register your dog, license it. How about a chip?"

Bob said, "What?"

Eric said, "A security chip. They implant them in the

dogs. Pooch goes missing, shows up at a vet, the vet scans the dog, up pops a bar code and all the owner's info. The owner, meanwhile, he's walking around with a slip of paper, has the security chip account number on it. Like this."

Eric pulled a small slip of paper out of his wallet and held it up so Bob could see it. Had the bar code on it and everything. He returned it to his wallet.

Eric said, "You got my dog, Bob."

"He's my dog."

Eric met his eyes and shook his head.

Bob carried Rocco across the kitchen. When he opened the crate, he could feel Eric Deeds's eyes on his back. He put Rocco inside the crate. Straightened. Turned back to Eric and said, "We're going now."

"We are?"

"Yeah."

Eric clapped his hands on his thighs and stood. "Then I guess we're going, aren't we?"

He and Bob walked down the dark hall and ended up in the foyer again.

Eric spied an umbrella in the stand to the right of the front door. He picked it up, looked at Bob. He slid the runner up and down the shaft a few times.

"You beat him," Bob said again because it seemed an important detail.

"But I'll tell the police *you* did." Eric continued to slide the runner back and forth, flapping the cover a bit.

Bob said, "What do you want?"

Eric gave that small private smile. He wrapped the strap around the umbrella until it was tight. He opened the front door. He looked out at the day, then back at Bob.

Eric said, "It's sunny now, but you never know."

When he reached the sidewalk, Eric Deeds took a big sniff of air and walked up the street under a bright sky with the umbrella under his arm.

CHAPTER 8

Rules and Regulations

Eric Deeds had been born and raised (if you could call it that) in East Buckingham, but he'd spent a few years away—hard years—before ending back in the house he'd grown up in a little over a year ago. For those few years he was gone, though, he'd been stuck in South Carolina.

He went down there to do a crime and the crime didn't work out too well, left a pawnshop owner with cranial bleeding and a speech impediment, got one of Eric's buddies shot dead and stupid-looking in the spring rain and Eric and the other buddy sent to Broad River Correctional to do three years.

Eric wasn't built for hard time, and his third day inside he got caught in the middle of a cafeteria riot where he raised his hands in fear and managed to block a shank in midflight, the blade going straight through his hand but not into the head of a guy named Padgett Webster.

Padgett was a drug dealer with Broad River respect. Padgett became Eric's protector. Even as he pushed Eric down on the mattress and entered his ass with a dick the length and width of a cucumber, Padgett assured Eric that he owed him. He wouldn't forget. Eric had to look him up when he got released, call in the marker, take something to get him started in the postprison life.

Padgett was kicked loose six months before Eric, and Eric had time alone to think about things. To consider his life, the corkscrew path that led him here. His one remaining buddy in the joint—Vinny Campbell, who came down here from Boston and got busted with him—added another year to his sentence for taking a hammer to another con's elbow in the carpentry shop. He did this on behalf of the Aryans, his new brothers, and they gave him a heroin habit as thanks, and Vinny barely talked to Eric anymore, just stumbled around with his skinhead crew, the droopy balloon bags under his eyes gone coffee-black.

At Broad River, they were the toys with the snapped limbs, the shorted battery wires, the exposed stuffing. Even if repaired, those toys were not welcomed back into the child's room.

Eric's only chance to make it in the world now was to create his own tablet of laws. Laws just for him. He did this one night in his cell, came up with a careful list of nine rules.

He wrote them down on a sheet of paper and folded that sheet and walked out of Broad River Correctional Institution with the sheet in his back pocket, the creases fuzzy and fat from constant unfolding and refolding.

THE DAY AFTER HE got out, Eric stole a car. He drove it to a Target off the interstate and swiped a Hawaiian shirt that was two sizes too big and a couple rolls of packing tape. He saved the little money he had to buy a gun off a guy whose name he'd been given in Broad River. Then he called Padgett from a pay phone outside of a motel in Bremeth and made arrangements, the heat wisping white off the black tar and dripping from the trees.

He sat the rest of the day in his room, remembering what the prison shrink had said—that he was not evil. His brain was not evil. He knew it wasn't; he spent a lot of time wandering its pink folds. It was just confused and hurt and filled with misshapen parts like an auto junkyard. Underexposed photographs, a greasy glass tabletop, a sink tucked kitty-corner between two cinder-block walls, his mother's vagina, two plastic chairs, a dimly lit bar, soiled maroon rags, a bowl of peanuts, a woman's lips saying *I do like you, I do,* a white swing seat of hard plastic, a disintegrating baseball spewing across a gray-blue sky, a sewer grate, a rat, two Charleston Chew bars clenched in one small, sweaty hand, a tall fence, a beige cotton dress tossed over the back of a vinyl car seat, a get-well card signed by the entire sixth grade, a wooden dock with the lake lapping underneath, a pair of damp sneakers.

The List was in his back pocket as he went up the back walk to Padgett's house at midnight. The trees dripped in the dark, dripped onto the cracked stone walkway with a soft, steady clatter. The whole state dripped. Everything was too moist in Eric's opinion. Squishy. Midnight, and he could feel moisture beading against the back of his neck, leaving dark patches in his shirt below the armpits.

He couldn't wait to get out of here. To put Broad River and banyan trees and the throat-clog scent of tobacco fields and textile mills and all these black people—black people everywhere, sullen and crafty and moving with a deceptive slowness—and the whole constant drip drip drip of the American South behind him.

Get back to cobblestone and an autumn bite in the night air and a decent fucking sub shop. Back to bars that didn't play country music and streets where every third vehicle wasn't a pickup and people didn't drawl so thick and slow you couldn't understand half of what they were saying.

Eric had come there to pick up a kilo of black tar heroin. Sell it up north, send the money back to Padgett on a sixty-forty split, the sixty being Padgett's, the forty Eric's, but still a good deal because Eric didn't have to front the price of the product. Padgett was just going to give it to him on trust, pay back his debt for what Eric did with his hand.

Padgett opened the door to a screened-in porch, and the

small shack creaked in a sliver of breeze that shimmied through the trees. The porch was lit by a green bulb and smelled of wet animal and Eric noticed a bag of charcoal propped up to the right of the door beside a rusted Hibachi and a cardboard box filled with empty wine coolers and fifths of Early Times.

Padgett said, "Ain't you a sight, boy?" and clapped him on the shoulder. Padgett was slim and hard and his muscles rippled with gristle. His hair, gone mostly to white, looked like snow on a coalfield, and he smelled of the heat and the banana-musk breeze. "A white sight at that. Ain't had one of your kind 'round here in a long time."

To get here, Eric had followed the main strip through the flyspeck town, took a right past the train tracks, left behind a stretch of three gas stations, one bar, and a 7-Eleven. He drove three miles through rutted streets hash-cut by dirt alleys, jungles of rotting eucalyptus spilling over abandoned shotgun shacks, the last white face somewhere back before the train tracks and a thousand years away. Maybe one working streetlight for every four blocks of sloping houses and dark-scrabble fields. Brothers standing on collapsed porches drinking 40s and smoking blunts, car heaps rusting through riotous stalks of grass, while ebony, high-boned sisters scuffled past cracked, uncovered windows, babies held to their shoulders. Midnight, and the whole place lethargically awake, waiting for someone to come turn off the heat.

He said to Padgett as they entered the house, "You got some humidity around here, man."

"Shit, yeah," the old man said. "We do got enough of that to go around. How you been, nigger?"

"Awright." They passed through a living room gone curled and rank in the heat, Eric remembering how Padgett used to lie on top of him after lights-out and whisper "My white little nigger" in his ear as his fingers clenched his hair.

"This here Monica," Padgett said as they entered the kitchen.

She sat by a table pressed lengthwise against the window, all blown-out features and knobby joints, eyes as wide and dead as a pair of sinkholes, skin stretched too tight for the bone underneath. Eric knew from conversations in his cell that she was Padgett's woman, mother of four kids long gone from here, and that just to the right of her hand was a sawed-off twelve-gauge hanging from hooks screwed to the underside of the table.

Monica took a sip from her wine cooler, grimaced in acknowledgment, went back to leafing through a magazine by her elbow.

Rule Number One, Eric thought. Remember Rule Number One.

"Don't mind her," Padgett said as he opened the fridge. "She all cranky 'tween about eleven pee-em and noon the next day." He handed Eric a can of Milwaukee's Best from a full battalion of them that filled the top shelf, took another out for himself, and shut the door.

"Monica," he said, "this the man I been telling you about, little nigger who saved my life. Show her your hand, man."

Eric raised his palm in front of her face, showed her the cabled knot of scars where the shank went straight through, came out the other side. Monica gave it a flick of a nod, and Eric dropped the hand. He still couldn't feel shit in there, though everything worked okay.

Monica turned her eyes back to her magazine, flipped a page. "I know who he is, old fool. You ain't shut up about that place since the day you walked out of it."

Padgett gave Eric a beam of a smile. "So how long you been out?"

"The day." Eric took a long sip of his beer.

They spent a few minutes talking about Broad River. Eric filled Padgett in on some of the power struggles he missed, most of them just noise, told him of the screw who shipped out on a medical when he pilfered the wrong con's stash, started thinking his skin had turned purple and tore off several fingernails scratching against a wall in the yard. Padgett pumped him for as much gossip as he could, and Eric remembered what an old hen Padgett had always been, sitting out every morning by the weight benches with the older cons, all of them cackling and dishing like they were on a talk show.

Padgett dumped their empties in a wastebasket and got them two more, handed Eric his. "I told you eighty-twenty on the split, right?"

Eric felt a bad vibe enter the room. "Told me sixty-forty."

Padgett leaned forward, eyes going wide. "And me fronting you the purchase? Nigger, you might have saved my life, but, shit . . ."

"Just telling you what you told me."

"What you *think* you *heard*," the old man said. "Nah, nah. It's going to be eighty-twenty. Send you walking out my door with a full key? Don't know if I'll see you again? That's a lot of trust, man. Damn truckload of trust."

"You got that right," Monica said, eyes on her magazine.

"Yeah. It's eighty-twenty." Padgett's happy eyes went small and unhappy. "We clear?"

"Sure," Eric said, feeling small, feeling white. "Sure, Padgett, that's fine."

Padgett beamed another of those hundred-watt smiles. "Yeah. I could say ninety-ten and really, what you gone do about it, nigger, am I right?"

Eric shrugged, drank some more beer, eyes on the sink.

"I said, 'Am I right?'"

Eric looked over at the old man. "You're right, Padgett."

Padgett nodded and banged his beer can off Eric's, took a swig.

Rule Number Two, Eric reminded himself. Don't ever forget that one. Not for one second in your whole life.

A slim guy in a multicolored cotton bathrobe and tan socks walked into the kitchen, sniffling, a wad of tissue held to his upper lip. Jeffrey, Eric figured, Padgett's baby brother. Padgett told him once that Jeffrey had killed five men that he *knew of*, said it didn't bother Jeffrey no more than taking a swim. Said if Jeffrey had a soul, they'd have to send out a search party for it.

Jeffrey had the dull eyes of a mole, and they rolled across Eric's face. "How you doing? You awright?"

Eric says, "I'm good. You?"

"I'm awright." Jeffrey dabbed his nose with the tissue. He sucked hard and wet through his nostrils, opened a cabinet above the sink and pulled down a bottle of Robitussin. He snapped off the cap with a flick of his thumb, tilted his head back, and drained half the bottle.

"How you feeling really?" This from Monica, eyes still on the magazine, but it was the first interest she'd shown in anything or anyone since Eric had come in the house.

"Not good," Jeffrey said. "Motherfucker got up in me, don't want to come out."

"Should have you some soup," Monica said. "Keep a blanket around you."

"Yeah," Jeffrey said. "Yeah, you right." He screwed the cap back on the Robitussin, put it back on the shelf.

Padgett said, "You talk to that nigger?"

"Which nigger?"

"One always down front the Pic-N-Pay."

Rules Number Three and Five, Eric repeated in his head like a mantra. Three and Five.

"I talked to him." Jeffrey sucked hard through his nose again, dabbed underneath it with the tissue.

"And?"

"And what? Nigger's the same place every day. He ain't going nowhere."

"Ain't him I'm worried about. His friends."

"Friends." Jeffrey shook his head. "That boo's friends ain't a problem."

"How you figure?"

Jeffrey coughed several times into the back of his hand, the hacks tearing up through his chest like cleavers pulled through a sea of hubcaps. He wiped his eyes and looked over at Eric, as if seeing him for the first time.

Saw something in Eric's face suddenly that he did not like.

He said to Padgett, "You pat this boy down?"

Padgett waved it away. "Aw, just look at him. He ain't up for no trouble."

Jeffrey hawked a load of phlegm into the sink. "You fucking up, old man. You slipping."

"Like I been saying," Monica said in a tired singsong, flipped another page.

"White boy." Jeffrey crossed the kitchen. "I got to pat you down, man."

Eric placed his beer on the corner of the stove top, held out his arms.

"Try not to give you my cold." Jeffrey stuffed the tissue paper in his bathrobe pocket. "You don't want the motherfucker, neither." His hands pressed against Eric's chest, then waist, testicles, the inside of his thighs and his ankles. "Fills your head tight. My throat feel like a motherfucking cat fell down it, started clawing its way back up." Jeffrey gave Eric's lower back a quick, confident feel-around, sniffled.

"Awright, you clean." He turned to Padgett. "That hard, old man?"

Padgett rolled his eyes at Jeffrey.

Eric scratched the back of his neck and wondered how many people had died in this house. As he had so often in prison, he marveled at how boring and basic the worst in people could be. The light above his head worked its way through his scalp, spread hot through his brain.

Jeffrey said, "Where that knottyhead at?"

Padgett pointed to a bottle of Seagram's gin on the shelf above the oven.

Jeffrey took it down, grabbed a glass. "Thought I told you about keeping it in the freezer. Like my shit cold, man."

Padgett said, "You need to get up on out of here, buy yourself a shawl. You become an old woman, Jeffrey."

The room swayed a bit as Eric scratched the back of his neck, his fingers going down behind his collar and then down between his shoulder blades. He felt hot and his head drummed and his mouth was dry. So dry. As if he'd never taste another drink till the day he died. He noticed his can of beer sitting where he put it when Jeffrey frisked him. He considered reaching for it, then decided he couldn't afford to.

"All I hear day in and day out, old man, is your mouth running. Running like fucking I-don't-know-what. But running."

Padgett drained his Old Mil', crushed it, and opened the fridge for another.

Jeffrey rested his drink on the side of the sink, turned to look at Eric, and said, "Nigger, *what*?" in a tone of deflated surprise as Eric pulled his hand free of the back of his shirt, produced a small .22 with a flap of packing tape still stuck to the barrel, the flesh by his upper spine tingling from where the tape ripped free. He shot Jeffrey just below the Adam's apple, and Jeffrey slid down against the counters below the sink.

He put the next one in the wall beside Monica's ear and she got her hand under the table, ducking, her chin between her thighs, and Eric fired a round through the top of her skull. For maybe a second, he paused, fascinated by the small hole that appeared in her head, as dark as any hole he'd ever seen, darker than her dark, dark hair. And then he turned.

His next shot knocked into Padgett, knocked the beer out of his hand and turned the man around, banged his hip and part of his head off the fridge door.

The echo of the gunshots made the whole room throb.

The gun in Eric's hand shook slightly, but not much, and the pounding in his head seemed to be going away.

Padgett, sitting on the floor, said, "You dumb piece of shit." His voice was high, girlish. He had a hole in the middle of his sweat-stained T-shirt that drizzled and kept growing wider.

Eric thought, I just shot three people. Man, oh, man.

He lifted the can of beer off the floor. He popped the tab

and it sprayed into a table leg. He placed it in Padgett's hand, watched the foam slide down and froth all over Padgett's wrist and fingers. Padgett's face turned the chalk of his hair. A distant whistle came from somewhere in his chest. Eric sat on the floor for a moment as Monica's body tipped out of its chair and thumped to the linoleum.

He ran his palm over the snowy coalfield atop Padgett's head. Even in his condition, Padgett half flinched, trying to back away. He had no place to go, though, and Eric rubbed his palm back and forth over the hair several times and then sat back again.

Padgett got a hand to the floor and tried to push himself up. The hand gave way and Padgett sat again. He gave it another try, reaching out blindly for a chair, finally getting the heel of his hand on the seat, tongue falling out of his mouth and hanging down over his lower lip as he gave himself a push up. He got to where he was half standing, knees bent and quaking, and then the chair slid away, and Padgett went back down, much harder this time, and sat there taking sharp, tiny breaths, mouth puckered, eyes on his lap.

"What made you think you could get the better of me?" Eric asked Padgett, and his own lips felt like rubber bands.

The old man took his tiny breaths, his eyes wide, his mouth open. He was trying to speak but all that came out was *whu, whu, whu.*

Eric leaned back to take aim. Padgett stared at the barrel, his eyes wild and caged. Eric let him get a good long look.

Padgett scrunched his eyes tight against the bullet he knew was coming.

Eric waited him out.

When he opened his eyes, Eric shot him in the face.

"Rule Number Seven." Eric stood. "Gotta move, gotta move."

He went under the stairs and into the back bedroom and opened the closet door. There was a safe there. It was about three feet tall and two feet wide and Eric knew from many late nights with Padgett in their cell that there was nothing inside but phone books. It wasn't even bolted to the floor. He pulled it out, grunting with the effort, wrestling it from side to side until it cleared the threshold and sat to the left of the door. He was left looking down at floorboards scratched and torn with divots. He lifted a slat and it came up easy. He tossed it behind him and lifted out four more and looked down at the stash— bags and bags of the black tar, tightly packed. He pulled out the bags one by one and placed them on the bed until the hiding place was empty. There were fourteen bags.

He looked around for a suitcase or gym bag, but there wasn't one and he went back to the kitchen. He had to step over Padgett's legs and Monica's head to open the doors under the sink. He found a box of trash bags there at the same moment it hit him that he'd left Jeffrey propped against these same doors, Jeffrey in his bathrobe and tan socks with the fucking bullet in his throat.

He noticed splashes and gouts of blood on the drawers to

his left and then others on the floor and on the door and the jamb leading into the hall. The spray patterns were fat red moths that he followed into the hall, where he expected to find Jeffrey on his belly, wheezing or dead.

But he wasn't there. The blood moths turned at the staircase and then disappeared in the darkness of the narrow, sagging steps and the faded, tattered rug in the center. A naked lightbulb hung from the low ceiling up top.

Standing there, he could hear a ragged breathing. It came from the right of that lightbulb, back in one of the rooms above him. He could hear a drawer being pulled open.

He swallowed against a flutter of panic. Rule Number Seven, Rule Number Seven. Don't think, do it. He backed out onto the porch quick and and grabbed the bag of charcoal he'd seen there. Match Light. No lighter fluid needed. They thought of everything these days.

In the hall again, he took it slow as he craned his head around the staircase, listening for the rattle of breath from an open throat. When he was sure there was no Jeffrey waiting on the dark stairs or at the top of them, he came around to the bottom step and laid the bag of charcoal there.

It took about thirty seconds to get the ends of the bag going, and he singed his thumb on the striking wheel of his Bic. Then, all at once, the flames got dancing. Someone must have spilled a shit-ton of liquor on the stairway runner over the years because the flames caught the edges of the faded rug and streaked up the stairs like runway lights. The carbon monoxide got to his head and he stepped back. The smoke was black and insane with that kerosene smell and Eric went to step around the fire, and a bullet chocked up the floor in front of him. Another bullet zipped past his head and hit the door to the porch.

Eric aimed past the fire and shot up into the darkness. A flash answered him back, several of them, and the bullets hit the walls and spit splinters into his hair.

He crouched against the wall. Flames licked his ear and he saw that his shoulder was on fire. He slapped at it until it went out, but now the wall was on fire. The wall, the staircase, the bedroom on the other side of the wall. Fuck. The heroin was in that bedroom, waiting on the bed.

The whole hallway was on fire now and the black billows of oily smoke tore at his eyes and lungs. He shot Jeffrey as Jeffrey jumped over the staircase railing and descended through the flames, a useless 9mm in his hand. Eric shot him again as he landed in the hallway and Jeffrey tipped back off his heels and into the fire, his bathrobe alive with it, one hand still grasping his open throat.

Eric tried to get around the fire, but it was pointless. It was everywhere now. And anywhere it wasn't was black with smoke.

Stupid, he thought. Eric, you're stupid. Stupid, stupid, stupid.

But not as stupid as the three dead assholes he was leaving behind.

Eric walked out the door and back up the cracked stone

walk with its ticking trees dripping and ticking, and he climbed in his car and drove out down the dirt road. He turned onto another road of cracked and rubbled tar, and he wondered how the hell people lived in such a shithole of a neighborhood. Get a fucking job, he thought. Lay off the crack. Get some self-respect or you're no better than gerbils. Yippy fucking gerbils in a shitty little cage.

Even if his plan had succeeded and he had walked back out of there with several kilos of black tar heroin, there was no guarantee he could have sold it. Who would he have sold it to? He didn't know anyone back in Boston who could move that kind of weight, and even if he was introduced to that type of person, they'd probably rip him off. Probably have to kill him while they were at it so he didn't come back at them.

So maybe it was just as well, but now he was heading home with no stake and no way to make money. Not that there wouldn't *be* a way to make money as long as he kept his eyes open and his ears to the ground. One good thing about shitty old East Buckingham, there was so much dirty money flowing in and out of that neighborhood on any given day— far more than any legitimate income—that a smart man just had to be patient.

He pulled out his list of rules, unfolded it with one hand, and propped it on his thigh to read as he drove. It was dark in the car, but he knew it by heart, didn't have to read it anymore really, just liked what it represented down there on his leg. In his handwriting, the letters carefully etched there—

1. *Never trust a convict.*
2. *No one loves you.*
3. *Shoot first.*
4. *Brush three times a day.*
5. *They'd do it to you.*
6. *Get fucking paid.*
7. *Work fast.*
8. *Always appear reasonable.*
9. *Get a dog.*

He took a left at the train tracks and saw the lights of the 7-Eleven ahead, thinking the trip down seemed twice as long as the trip back, and how it was weird that it usually worked like that, and then he thought: Nadia.

I wonder what she's up to these days.

CHAPTER 9

Stay

THEY HADN'T SEEN RARDY since the robbery. He'd been discharged from the hospital the next day, they knew that much, but from there he'd gone ghost. They talked it over in the empty bar one morning, half the chairs still up on the tables and the bar top.

Cousin Marv said, "It ain't like him."

Bob had the paper spread on the bar before him. It was official—the archdiocese had announced the closing of Saint Dominic's Church in East Buckingham, a closing the cardinal had described as "imminent."

Bob said, "He's missed days before."

Cousin Marv said, "Not in a row, not without calling."

THERE WERE TWO PICTURES of Saint Dom's in the paper, one taken recently, the other a hundred years ago. Same sky above. But no one who'd been under the first sky was still alive for the second. And maybe they were glad not to have had to stick around in a world so unrecognizable from the one they entered. When Bob had been a kid, your parish was your country. Everything you needed and needed to know was contained within it. Now that the archdiocese had shuttered half the parishes to pay for the crimes of the kid-diddler priests, Bob couldn't escape the fact that those days of parish dominion, long dwindling, were gone. He was a certain type of guy, of a certain half-generation, an almost generation, and while there were still plenty of them left, they were older, grayer, they had smoker's coughs, they went in for checkups and never checked back out.

"I dunno," Marv was saying. "This Rardy thing's got me keyed up, I don't mind telling you. I mean, I got guys after me and—"

Bob said, "You don't have guys *after you*."

Cousin Marv said, "What'd I tell you about the guy in the car?"

Bob said, "He asked you directions."

Cousin Marv said, "But it was the way he did it, the look he was giving me. And what about this guy with the umbrella?"

Bob said, "That's about the dog."

Cousin Marv said, " 'The dog.' How do you know?"

Bob stared into the unlit sections of the barroom and felt death all around him, a side effect, he believed, of the robbery and that poor guy in the back of the van. The shadows became hospital beds, stooped old men shopping for sympathy cards, empty wheelchairs.

"Rardy's just sick," Bob said eventually. "He'll turn up."

BUT A COUPLE OF hours later, with Marv holding down the bar for the hard-core day drinkers, Bob walked over to Rardy's place, a second-floor apartment sandwiched between two others in a weary three-decker on Perceval.

Bob sat in the living room with Moira, Rardy's wife. She'd been a really pretty girl once, Moira, but life with Rardy and a kid with some kind of learning disabilities sucked the pretty out of her like sugar up a straw.

Moira said, "I ain't seen him in days."

Bob said, "Days, uh?"

She nodded. "He drinks a lot more than he lets on."

Bob sat forward, the surprise showing on his face.

"I know, right?" she said. "He hides it pretty good but he's maintenance nipping from the time he's up in the AM."

Bob said, "I've seen him take a *drink*."

"The little airplane bottles?" Moira said. "He keeps them in his coat. So, I dunno, he could be with his brothers or some of his old friends from Tuttle Park."

"When's the last time?" Bob asked.

"I saw him? Couple days. Prick's done this to me before, though."

"You try calling him?"

Moira sighed. "He don't answer his cell."

The kid appeared in the doorway, still wearing pajamas at three in the afternoon. Patrick Dugan, nine or ten, couldn't remember which. He gave Bob a blank gaze, even though they'd met a hundred times, then looked at his mother, all itchy, thin shoulders bouncing.

"You said," Patrick said to his mother. "I need help."

"All right. Let me finish talking to Bob here."

"You said, you said, you said. I need help. I need it."

"And, honey?" Moira closed her eyes for a brief moment then opened them. "I said I'd be right there and I will. Just show me like we talked about, that you can work by yourself a couple more minutes."

"You said, though." Patrick bounced from one foot to the other in the doorway. "You said."

"Patrick." Moira's voice was tight with warning now.

Patrick let loose a howl, his face an unattractive blend of fury and fear. It was a primal sound, a zoo sound, a wail at limited gods. His face turned the red of a sunburn and the cords in his neck stood out. And the howl unfurled and went on and on. Bob looked at the floor, looked out the window, tried to act natural. Moira just looked tired.

Then the kid clamped his mouth shut and ran away down the hall.

Moira unwrapped a stick of gum and put it in her mouth.

She offered the pack to Bob and he thanked her as he took one and they sat there in silence and chewed gum.

Moira jerked her thumb at the doorway where her son had stood. "Rardy would tell ya that's why he drinks. They told us Patrick has HDHD? And/or ADD. And/or cognitive disso-something-something. My mother says he's just an asshole. I dunno. He's my kid."

"Sure," Bob said.

"You okay?"

"Me?" Bob sat back a bit. "Yeah, why?"

"You're different."

"How?"

Moira shrugged as she stood. "I dunno. You're taller or something. You see Rardy? Tell him we need 409 and Tide."

She went to see her son. Bob let himself out.

NADIA AND BOB SAT on the swings in the empty playground in Pen' Park. Rocco lay at their feet in the sand, a tennis ball in his mouth. Bob glanced at the scar on Nadia's neck, and she caught him as he looked away.

"You never ask about it. Only person I ever met didn't ask about it in like the first five minutes."

Bob said, "Not my business. It's yours."

Nadia said, "Where are you from?"

Bob looked around. "I'm from here."

"No, I mean, what planet?"

Bob smiled and shook his head. He finally understood what people were talking about when they said "tickled pink." That's about how she made him feel—from a distance, in his mind, or, like now, sitting close enough to touch (though they never had)—tickled pink.

He said, "People used to use the telephone in public? They went into a booth, they closed the door. Or they talked as softly as they could. Now? People talk about their, ya know, their bowel movements while they're having them in a public restroom. I don't understand."

Nadia laughed.

"What?"

"Nothing. No." She raised a hand in apology. "I've just never seen you get worked up. I'm not even sure I follow. What's a pay phone have to do with my scar?"

"No one," Bob said, "respects privacy anymore. Everyone wants to tell you every fucking thing about themselves. Excuse me. I'm sorry. I shouldn't have said that word. You're a lady."

She smiled an even broader smile. "Keep going."

He raised a hand by his ear and didn't notice until he had. He lowered it. "Everyone wants to tell you something—anything, everything—about themselves and they just go on and on and on. But when it comes time to *show* you who they are? Their shit is weak, Nadia. Their shit is lacking. And they just cover it up by talking more, by explaining away what can't be explained away. And then they go on talking more shit about someone else. That make sense?"

Her big smile had turned into a small one, curious and unreadable at the same time. "I'm not sure."

He caught himself licking his upper lip, an old nervous habit. He wanted her to understand. He needed her to understand. He'd never wanted anything so much that he could remember.

"Your scar?" he said. "That's yours. You'll tell me about it when you'll tell me. Or you won't. Either way."

He looked out at the channel for a bit. Nadia patted his hand once and looked out at the channel too and they stayed that way for some time.

BEFORE WORK, BOB DROPPED by Saint Dom's and sat in an empty pew in the empty church and took it all in.

Father Regan entered the altar off the sacristy, mostly in street clothes, though his trousers were black. He watched Bob sit there for a bit.

Bob asked, "Is it true?"

Father Regan walked down the center aisle. He took the pew ahead of Bob's. Turned and slung his arm over the back. "The diocese feels we could better meet our pastoral commitments if we merged with Saint Cecilia's, yeah."

Bob said, "But they're selling *this* church," and pointed down at his own pew.

Father Regan said, "This building and the school will be sold, yeah."

Bob looked up at the soaring ceilings. He'd been looking up at them since he was three years old. He'd never known the ceilings in any other church. That's how it was supposed to be until the day he died. How it had been for his father, how it had been for his father's father. Some things—a few rare things—were supposed to stay what they'd always been.

Bob said, "You?"

Father Regan said, "I haven't been reassigned yet."

Bob said, "They protect the kid-diddlers and the douche bags who covered up for them but they haven't figured out what to do with you? That's fucking wise."

Father Regan gave Bob a look like he wasn't sure he'd met *this* Bob before. And maybe he hadn't.

Father Regan said, "Is everything else okay?"

"Sure." Bob looked at the transepts. Not for the first time he wondered how they'd had the wherewithal back in 1878— or 1078, for that matter—to build them. "Sure, sure, sure."

Father Regan said, "I understand you've become friends with Nadia Dunn."

Bob looked at him.

"She's had some trouble in the past." Father Regan patted the top of the pew lightly. The pat turned into an absent caress. "Some would say, *she* is troubled."

The silent church towered over them, beating like a third heart.

Bob said, "Do you have friends?"

Father Regan's eyebrows arched. "Sure."

Bob said, "I don't mean just, like, other priests. I mean, like, buddies. People you can, I dunno, be around."

Father Regan nodded. "Yeah, Bob. I do."

"I don't," Bob said. "I mean, I didn't."

Bob looked around the church some more. He gave Father Regan a smile. He said, "God bless," and left the pew.

Father Regan said, "God bless."

Bob stopped at the baptismal font on his way out the door. He blessed himself. He stood there with his head down. Then he blessed himself a second time and left through the center doors.

CHAPTER 10

Whoever Is Holy

COUSIN MARV STOOD IN the doorway to the alley, smoking, while Bob gathered up the empty trash barrels from the night before. As usual, the barrels had been tossed all over the alley by the garbage truck guys and Bob had to range a bit to get them.

Cousin Marv said, "It's too much for them to just put them back down where they found them. That would require courtesy."

Bob stacked two plastic barrels together, brought them over to the back wall. He noticed, propped against the wall between the barrels and a rat trap, a black plastic trash bag, the kind used on construction sites, extra heavy duty. He hadn't left it there. He was familiar enough with the businesses on either side of them—Nails Saigon and Doctor Sanjeev K Seth—to know what their trash usually looked like, and this wasn't it. He left the bag there a moment and went into the alley for the last barrel.

Bob said, "If you'd just pay for a Dumpster—"

Cousin Marv said, "Why should I pay for a Dumpster? I don't own the bar anymore, remember? 'Pay for a Dumpster.' Ain't your bar Chovka took."

Bob said, "That was ten years ago."

Cousin Marv said, "Eight and a half."

Bob brought the last barrel to the wall. He walked over to the black plastic bag. It was a forty-five-gallon bag, but far from full. Whatever was inside wasn't big, but the bag jutted at the sides, so whatever was inside was a foot to eighteen inches long. A length of pipe, perhaps, or the kind of cardboard tubing posters came in.

Cousin Marv said, "Dottie thinks we should visit Europe. That's what I've become, kinda guy goes to Europe with his sister, hops on fucking tour buses with a camera around my neck."

Bob stood over the bag. It had been knotted at the top, but knotted so loosely it would take nothing but a light tug for the bag to open like a rose.

"Back in the day," Cousin Marv said, "I wanted to go on a trip, I went with Brenda Mulligan or Cheryl Hodge or, or, remember Jillian?"

Bob took another step closer to the bag. Now he stood so close that the only way to get closer would have been to climb in. "Jillian Waingrove. She was pretty."

"She was fucking smoking. We went together that whole summer? Used to go to that outdoor bar in Marina Bay. What was that called?"

Bob heard himself say, "The Tent," as he opened the bag and looked in. His lungs filled with lead and his head filled with helium. He turned away from the bag for a moment and the alley canted to the right.

"The Tent," Marv was saying. "Right, right. That still there?"

"Yeah," Bob heard himself say, his voice reaching his ears like something from a tunnel, "but they call it something else now."

He looked over his shoulder at Marv, let Marv see it in his eyes.

Cousin Marv flicked his cigarette into the alley. "What?"

Bob stood where he was, the flaps of the bag in his hand. An odor of decomposition floated out of the bag, a smell similar to raw chicken parts left in the sun.

Cousin Marv looked toward the bag then back at Bob. He remained in the doorway.

Bob said, "You need to—"

Cousin Marv said, "No, I don't."

Bob said, "What?"

Cousin Marv said, "I don't need to do anything. Okay? I'm standing right fucking here. I'm standing here because—"

Bob said, "You need to see—"

"I don't need to see anything! You hear me?" Cousin Marv said, "I don't need to see Europe or fucking Thailand or fucking whatever's in that bag. I'm standing right here."

"Marv."

Marv shook his head violently, the way a child would.

Bob waited.

Cousin Marv wiped at his eyes, suddenly embarrassed. "We were a crew once. 'Member that? People were afraid of us."

Bob said, "Yeah."

Marv lit another cigarette. He walked toward the bag the way you'd approach a stunned raccoon in the corner of your basement.

He reached Bob. He looked in the bag.

An arm, hacked off just below the elbow, lay in a small pile of bloody money. The arm sported a wristwatch that was stopped at six-fifteen.

Cousin Marv exhaled slowly and kept at it until there was no breath left in his lungs.

Cousin Marv said, "Well, that's just . . . I mean . . ."

"I know."

"It's . . ."

"I know," Bob said.

"It's obscene."

Bob nodded. "We gotta do something with it."

Cousin Marv said, "The money? Or the . . . ?"

Bob said, "I'm betting the money adds up to whatever we lost that night."

Cousin Marv said, "So, okay . . ."

Bob said, "So we give the money back to them. It's what they expect."

"And that?" Marv pointed at the arm. "*That?*"

"We can't just leave it here," Bob said. "It'll bring that cop right down on us."

"But we didn't do anything."

"Not this time," Bob said. "But how do you think Chovka or Papa Umarov are going to feel about us if the cops take a special interest?"

"Yeah," Marv said. "Sure, sure."

"Need you to focus, Marv."

Marv blinked at that. "You need *me* to focus?"

"Yeah, I do," Bob said and carried the bag inside.

IN THE TINY KITCHEN, next to the four-burner grill and the deep fryer, was a prep station where they made the sandwiches. Bob laid some wax paper on the counter. He pulled shrink-wrap from a dispenser above the counter. He lifted the arm out of the sink where he'd rinsed it and rolled it in the shrink wrap. When it was tightly wrapped, he placed it in the wax paper.

Marv watched from the doorway, a look of repulsion on his stricken face.

Cousin Marv said, "Like you've done this a thousand times."

Bob shot him a look. Cousin Marv blinked and looked at the floor.

Cousin Marv said, "You wonder if you hadn't mentioned the watch, maybe—"

"No," Bob said, a little sharper than he meant to. "I don't."

Cousin Marv said, "Well, I do."

Bob taped the edges of the wax paper, and the arm was now somewhat disguised as maybe an expensive pool cue or a foot-long sub. Bob put it in a gym bag.

He and Marv exited the kitchen into the bar and found Eric Deeds sitting there, hands folded on the bar top, just a guy waiting for a drink.

Marv and Bob both kept moving forward.

Cousin Marv said, "We're closed."

Eric said, "You got any Zima?"

"Who would we serve it to?" Marv asked. "Moesha?"

Bob and Cousin Marv came around the back of the bar, stared at Deeds.

Eric stood. "Your door was unlocked, so I thought . . ."

Marv and Bob looked at each other.

"No offense," Cousin Marv said to Eric Deeds, "but get the fuck out of here."

"Definitely no Zima?" Eric walked to the door. "Good seeing you, Bob." He waved. "You give Nadia my best, brutha."

Eric walked out. Marv ran to the door and threw the lock.

Cousin Marv said, "We're tossing the missing piece of the One-Armed Man back and forth like a fucking Hacky Sack, and the fucking door's unlocked."

Bob said, "Well, nothing happened."

"But it could have." He took a breath. "You know that kid?"

Bob said, "That's the guy I told you about."

"One claims the dog was his?"

"Yeah."

"He's fucked in the squash, that one."

Bob said, "You know him?"

Cousin Marv nodded. "He's from Mayhew Street. Saint Cecilia's Parish. You're old school—somebody ain't from your parish, they might as well be fucking Flemish. Kid's a piece of shit. Been to the joint a couple times, did a thirty-day in the cuckoo house, if I recall. The whole fucking Deeds family shoulda been Baker Acted a generation ago." Cousin Marv said, "Word around a few campfires is he's the one killed Glory Days."

Bob said, "I heard that, yeah."

Cousin Marv said, "Dispersed him from the planet Earth. That's what they say."

"Well . . ." Bob said, and then, with nothing left to say, he took the gym bag and walked out the back door.

After he left, Marv filled the bar sink with the bloody money. He engaged the tonic water button on the soda dispensing gun and sprayed the money.

He stopped. He stared at all that runny blood.

"Animals," he whispered and closed his eyes to all that blood. "Fucking savages."

AT PEN' PARK, BOB threw a stick and Rocco charged up the path for it. He brought it back, dropped it in front of Bob, and Bob threw it again, putting everything he had into it. While Rocco raced down the path, Bob reached into the gym bag and grabbed the packaged arm. He turned toward the channel and threw the arm like a tomahawk. He watched it arc high and tumble end over end before it reached its zenith in the sky and dropped quickly. It landed in the middle of the channel with a splash bigger than Bob would have predicted. Louder too. So loud he expected the cars driving past on the roadway on the opposite bank to all stop. But none did.

Rocco returned with the stick.

Bob said, "Good boy."

Bob threw the stick again and it bounced on the asphalt and then off the path. Rocco bounded across the park.

Bob heard tires behind him. He turned, expecting to see one of the park ranger pickup trucks, but instead it was Detective Torres driving toward him. Bob had no idea if he'd seen anything. Torres stopped and he got out of his car and approached Bob.

Torres said, "Hey, Mr. Saginowski." He glanced at the empty bag at Bob's feet. "We haven't caught them yet."

Bob stared at him.

"The guys who robbed your bar."

"Oh."

Torres laughed. "You remember, don't you?"

"Of course."

"Or have you been robbed so many times it all just blends together?"

Rocco ran up to them, dropped the stick, panted. Bob threw the stick and Rocco ran off again.

"No," Bob said. "I remember."

"Good. So, yeah, we haven't found them."

Bob said, "I assumed."

Torres said, "You assumed we didn't do our job?"

Bob said, "No. I always heard robberies were hard to arrest on."

Torres said, "So what I do for a living is pointless, what you're saying."

There was no way to win in this conversation so Bob just clammed up.

After a while, Torres said, "What's with the bag?"

Bob said, "I keep leashes and balls and poop bags in there and stuff."

Torres said, "It's empty."

Bob said, "Used my last poop bag, lost a ball."

Rocco trotted up, dropped the stick. Bob threw it and the dog took off again.

Torres said, "Richie Whelan."

Bob asked, "What about him?"

Torres asked, "You remember him?"

Bob said, "His friends were in the bar last week toasting the anniversary."

Torres asked, "What anniversary?"

Bob said, "The last time anyone ever saw him."

Torres said, "Which was at your bar."

Bob said, "Yeah, he left. Walked off to score some weed, I always heard."

Torres nodded. "You know an Eric Deeds? Blond guy?"

Bob said, "I don't know. I mean, maybe, but it's not ringing a bell."

Torres said, "He supposedly had some words with Whelan earlier that day."

Bob gave Torres a helpless smile and a matching shrug.

Torres nodded and kicked at a pebble with the toe of his shoe. "'Whoever is holy, let him approach.'"

Bob said, "'Scuse me?"

Torres said, "Church's position on who can receive Communion. If you're in a state of grace, have at it. If not, repent and *then* have at it. But you still don't take the sacrament. You forget to repent for something, Mr. Saginowski?"

Bob said nothing. He threw the stick for Rocco again.

Torres said, "See, me, I fuck up most days. It's a hard path to walk. End of the day, though, I go to confession. It's better'n therapy or AA. Come clean with God, next morning, receive Him at Holy Communion. You, though? Not so much."

Rocco brought back the stick, and this time it was Torres who picked it up. He held it in his hand for quite a while until Rocco started to whine. It was a high-pitched sound, one Bob had never heard before. But then he wasn't in the habit of taunting his dog. Just as he was about to grab the stick from Torres's hand, the cop cocked his arm and released the stick into the air. Rocco took off after it.

Torres said, "Meaningful penance, Mr. Saginowski—you should give it some thought. Good-looking dog."

He walked off.

CHAPTER 11

All Die

AFTER TORRES LEFT, BOB walked through the park for a bit but couldn't really remember much of it before he and Rocco found themselves back by his car. He felt so light-headed he wasn't sure he trusted himself to drive, so he stood by the car with his dog and looked at the hard winter sky, the sun trapped behind a wall of gray as thick as terry cloth. A few months from now, if the arm floated up somewhere along these banks, would Torres make the connection? Would he come for Bob then?

He's already coming for you now.

Bob took a long breath, held it, and then exhaled. This time, it didn't make him dizzy or pop the air in front of his face.

He told himself it was all going to work out. It was.

He got in his car and looked at himself in the visor mirror and said it out loud. "It's going to be fine."

Not that he believed it, but what were you gonna do?

He drove into Saint Dom's Parish and over to his house to drop Rocco off. As they got out of the car, Nadia exited the house.

Nadia said, "I came by to give him his afternoon walk. I freaked. Your cell on?"

Bob looked at his cell. "On vibrate. I didn't feel it."

"I called a bunch of times."

His screen read *Missed Call Nadia (6)*. "I see that now."

She cocked her head slightly. "I thought you were working today."

Bob said, "I am. I just . . . Yeah. It's too long a story to go into. But I should have called you. I'm sorry."

"Oh, no, no. Don't worry about it."

Bob came up on the porch with Rocco, who rolled over at Nadia's feet. She scratched his chest.

Bob said, "You know an Eric Deeds?"

Nadia kept her head down and continued scratching Rocco's chest. "I don't *know-him*-know-him, but I know him. You know, from around."

Bob said, "The way he said it, I figured you—"

"Figured I what?"

"Nothing. No. I don't know what I—"

Now she looked at him. Looked at him with something

in her eyes he'd never seen before. Something that told him to turn and run as fast as he could.

"Why're you on my ass about it?"

"What? I just asked a question."

She said, "You were insinuating."

"No, I wasn't."

"Now you're just arguing with me to argue with me."

"I'm not."

She rose from her knees. "See? I don't need this shit. Okay?"

Bob said, "Wait. What happened here?"

"You think you can just push me around, think you found a speed bag to tap-tap-tap with your big fist?"

"What?" Bob said. "Jesus. No."

She went to walk past him. Bob started to reach for her and then thought better of it, but it was too late.

"Don't you fucking *touch* me."

He took a step back from her. She pointed her finger in his face and then walked down the stairs, double-time.

On the sidewalk, she looked up at him. "Asshole," she said, her eyes brimming.

She walked away.

Bob stood there with zero idea how he managed to fuck up this big.

ONCE HE GOT BACK to the bar, Bob stayed in the back for an hour with a hair dryer and the wet money. When he came out, the bar was still mostly empty, just a few old-timers drinking bottom-shelf rye down the end closest to the door. Cousin Marv and Bob stood down the other end.

Bob said, "I just asked a question and everything went, like, sideways."

Cousin Marv said, "You could hand them the Hope Diamond, they'd complain about the weight." He turned a page of the paper. "You're sure he didn't see anything?"

"Torres?" Bob said, "Positive." Though he wasn't.

The front door opened and Chovka entered followed by Anwar. They passed the three old guys and came down the bar and took stools by Cousin Marv and Bob. They sat. They put their elbows on the bar. They waited.

The three old guys—Pokaski, Limone, and Imbruglia—didn't even have a conversation about it before they all left their stools at the same time and wandered off by the pool table.

Cousin Marv wiped down the bar by Chovka even though he'd wiped it down a minute before they came through the door. "Hi."

Chovka ignored him. He looked at Anwar. They both looked back at Bob and Cousin Marv. Chovka dug in his pocket. Anwar dug in his. Their hands came back out of their coats. They placed cigarette packs and lighters on the bar.

Bob rummaged under the bar and returned with the ashtray he kept there for Millie. He placed it between them. They lit their cigarettes.

Bob said, "Get you a drink, Chovka?"

Chovka smoked. Anwar smoked.

Bob said, "Marv."

Cousin Marv asked, "What?"

Bob said, "Anwar drinks Stella."

Cousin Marv went to the beer cooler. Bob pulled a bottle of Midleton Irish whiskey off the top shelf. He poured a healthy glass and placed it in front of Chovka. Cousin Marv returned with a Stella Artois and placed it by Anwar. Bob grabbed a coaster and lifted the beer, placed the coaster under it. Then he pulled a manila envelope out from under the register and placed it on the bar.

Bob said, "The bills are still a little damp, so I wrapped them in a Ziploc. But it's all there."

Chovka said, "A Ziploc."

Bob nodded. "I was going to, you know, toss it in a dryer, but we don't have one here, but I did the best I could with a hair dryer. But if you spread it all out on a table? They should all be crisp come morning."

"How'd it get wet in the first place?"

"We had to clean it," Bob said.

"Something on it?" Chovka's eyes were very still.

"Yes," Bob said.

Chovka considered the drink Bob had placed in front of him. "This isn't what you gave me last time."

Bob said, "That was the Bowmore 18. You thought it tasted like cognac. I think you'll like this more."

Chovka held the glass up to the light. He sniffed it. Looked at Bob. He put the glass to his lips and took a sip. He placed the glass on the bar. "We die."

"'Scuse me?" Bob said.

"All of us," Chovka said. "We die. So many different ways this happens. Anwar, did you know your grandfather?"

Anwar drank half his Stella in one gulp. "No. He's dead long time."

"Bob," Chovka said, "is your grandfather still alive? Either of them?"

"No, sir."

"But they lived full lives?"

"One died in his late thirties," Bob said, "the other made it into his sixties."

"But they lived on this earth. They fucked and fought and made babies. They thought *their* day was *the* day, the last word. And then they died. Because we die." He took another sip of his drink and repeated, "We die," in a soft whisper. "But before you do?" He turned on his stool and handed Anwar the glass. "You gotta try this fucking whiskey, man."

He slapped Anwar on the back. He laughed.

Anwar took a sip. He handed the glass back. "It's good."

"'It's good.'" Chovka snorted. "You don't understand the finer things, Anwar. That is your problem. Drink your beer." Chovka drained the rest of the glass, eyes locked on Cousin Marv. Then on Bob. "You understand the finer things, Bob."

"Thank you."

"I think you understand many more things than you let on."

Bob said nothing.

Chovka said, "You'll handle the drop."

Cousin Marv asked, "Tonight?"

Chovka shook his head.

They waited.

Chovka said, "Super Bowl."

And he and Anwar pushed off the bar. They scooped up their cigarettes and lighters. They walked down the bar and out the door.

Bob and Cousin Marv stood there, Bob again feeling so light-headed he wouldn't have been surprised to wake up on the floor ten minutes from now with no recollection of how he got there. The room didn't spin exactly, but it keep dimming and brightening, dimming and brightening.

Marv said, "You notice he never once referred to me, directed a question or comment my way? Only time he ever looked at me it was like I was a bit of toilet paper still stuck in his ass, he had to do another reach around."

"I didn't get that at all."

"You didn't get it at all because you were all fucking chummy with him. 'Here's your mint julep, massah, and forgive me if it doesn't taste like the eighteen-fucking-year-old cognac I gave you last time you checked up on us field slaves.' You fucking kidding me? He's going to fucking kill me."

"No, he's not. You're not making sense."

"I'm making perfect sense. He thinks me and dead fucking Rardy—"

"Rardy's not dead."

"Really? You seen him around lately?" He pointed at the door, whisper-hissing. "That fucking Chechen thinks me and Rardy hatched this thing with the One-Armed Corpse. You, he thinks you're too stupid or too fucking, I dunno, *nice* to rob him. But me, he gives the death stare."

"If he thought you had his five thousand, where'd he get the five grand in the bag from?"

"What?"

"The guys who stuck us up stole five grand. There was five grand in the bag with the"— he looked over by the pool table, made sure the three old guys were still there—"hand. So he found his money with the kid and he sent it back to us."

"Yeah?"

"Which means he can't think you have it if he sent it to us and we just gave it back to him."

"He can think I put the stickup guys up to it and they were holding the cash while I waited for things to cool down. And even if he doesn't think that, it's in his head, now that I'm a piece of shit. I'm not to be trusted. And guys like that don't ask if their opinions are *rational*. They just decide one day you're a flea and tomorrow's Flea Killing Day."

"Are you listening to yourself?"

Marv's face was beaded with sweat. "They're gonna use this place for a Super Sunday drop. Then they're gonna knock it over and either shoot us or leave us to live long enough for all the other crazy Chechneyans and fucking Georgians who put their money in our safe that night to decide we orchestrated it. And then they're going to work on us in some basement for three or four days until we don't have eyes or ears or fucking balls and all our teeth are smashed in. And then? Two in the hat, Bob. Two in the hat."

He came out from behind the bar.

"Marv."

Cousin Marv waved it off, started walking toward the door.

Bob said, "I can't work a Thursday night alone."

"Call BarTemps."

"Marv!"

Marv raised his arms in a "Whatta ya gonna do?" gesture and pushed the door open on the day. The door closed behind him and Bob stood behind the bar, the old-timers looking at him from over by the pool table before they went back to their drinks.

AT THE END OF a long night, Bob came up the street to find Nadia standing on his front porch, smoking. Bob could feel his own face light up like the Fourth of July.

Bob said, "You'll freeze out here."

She shook her head. "I just came out to smoke. I've been in with Rocco."

Bob said, "I don't care if you knew him. I don't care. He told me to say hi to you, like it meant something."

Nadia said, "What else he say?"

Bob said, "He said Rocco is his."

She flicked her cigarette into the street. Bob held the door open for her and she entered the house.

In the kitchen, he let Rocco out of his crate and plopped him on his lap at the table. Nadia took two beers out of the fridge, slid one to Bob.

They drank for a while in silence.

Nadia said, "So, Eric's cute, right? One night that was enough. I mean, I knew all the stories about him being fucked in the head, but then he left town for a while and when he came back he seemed calmer, like he'd pocketed his demons, you know? Boxed them up. For a while it seemed like he was different. Then when the crazy bus came to town, I was already in for a penny."

Bob said, "That's why your barrel."

Nadia looked at Rocco and shook her head. "No. We haven't been . . . together in, like, a year." She shook her head some more, trying to convince herself. Then: "So he beat Rocco, thinks he's dead, and he throws him into my trash, so I'll what?"

Bob said, "Think about him? I dunno."

Nadia processed that. "That does sound like Eric. Christ, I'm sorry."

Bob said, "You didn't know."

Nadia knelt in front of Bob and Rocco. She took the dog's head in her hand.

Nadia said, "Rocco. I'm not up on my saints. What's Rocco the saint of?"

Bob said, "Dogs. Patron saint of dogs."

Nadia said, "Well, yeah."

Bob said, "And pharmacists, bachelors, and the falsely accused."

Nadia said, "Dude has a full plate." She raised her beer in toast. "Well, shit, here's to Saint Rocco."

They toasted.

She took her seat again and ran the edge of her thumb along her scar. "You ever think some things you do are beyond, I dunno, forgiveness?"

Bob said, "From who?"

Nadia pointed up. "You know."

Bob said, "I get days, yeah, I think some sins you can't come back from. No matter how much good you do after, the devil's just waiting for your body to quit 'cause he already owns your soul. Or maybe there's no devil but you die and God says, 'Sorry, you can't come in. You did an unforgivable; you gotta be alone now. Forever.'"

Nadia said, "I'd take the devil."

"Right?" Bob said, "Other times? I don't think God's the problem. It's us, you know?"

She shook her head.

Bob said, "We don't let ourselves out of our own cages."

He wagged Rocco's paw at her. She smiled, drank her beer.

"I heard Cousin Marv doesn't own the bar. But some hard guys do. But you're not a hard guy. So why do you work there?"

Bob said, "Me and Cousin Marv go way back. He's actually my cousin. Him and his sister, Dottie. My mother and their father were sisters."

Nadia laughed. "Did they share makeup?"

"What'd I say? No, I meant, you know what I meant." He laughed. It was a real laugh and he couldn't remember the last time he'd had one of those. "Why you giving me shit?"

Nadia said, "It's fun."

The silence was beautiful.

Bob broke it eventually. "Marv thought he was a hard guy once. He had a crew for a while and we made some money, you know."

Nadia said, "But you don't have a crew anymore?"

Bob said, "You gotta be mean. Tough ain't enough. These mean crews started coming around. And we blinked."

Nadia said, "But you're still in the life."

Bob shook his head. "I just tend bar."

She looked at him carefully over her beer and let him see that she didn't really believe him but she wouldn't press.

Nadia said, "You think he'll just go away?"

"Eric?" he said. "Doesn't strike me as the type."

"He's not. He killed a kid named Glory Days. Well, that wasn't his—"

Bob said, "Richie Whelan, yeah."

Nadia nodded. "Eric killed him."

Bob said, "Why?"

"I dunno. He's not a big fan of why, Eric." She stood. "Another beer?"

Bob hesitated.

"Come on, Bob, let your hair down."

Bob beamed. "Why not?"

Nadia put another beer in front of him. She ruffled Rocco's head. She sat and they drank.

BOB WALKED NADIA TO her front stoop. " 'Night."

" 'Night, Bob. Thanks."

"For what?"

She shrugged. She put her hand on his shoulder and gave his cheek a quick peck. Then she was gone.

BOB WALKED HOME. THE streets were silent. He came upon a long patch of ice on the sidewalk. Instead of walking around it, he slid on it, arms out for balance. Like a little kid. When he reached the end of the patch, he smiled up at the stars.

BACK AT HOME, HE cleared the beer cans from the table. He rinsed them and placed them in a plastic bag hanging from a drawer handle. He smiled at Rocco, who was curled up and sleeping in the corner of his crate. He shut off the kitchen light.

He turned the kitchen light back on. He opened the crate. Rocco opened his eyes, stared at him. Bob considered the new addition to Rocco's crate:

The umbrella Eric Deeds took from the house.

Bob removed it from the crate and sat with it for a long time.

CHAPTER 12

Like No Time at All

ERIC DEEDS SAT IN the back of Hi-Fi Pizza with a couple slices late on Friday morning. Eric always sat near the back of any-place he ate or drank. He liked to always be no more than ten feet from an exit. In case, he'd told a girl once.

"In case what?"

"In case they come for me."

"Who's they?"

"There's always a they," Eric had said, looking in her eyes—this was Jeannie Madden he was dating at the time—and he thought he saw real understanding looking back at him. Finally—fucking *finally*—someone who got him.

She caressed his hand. "There is always a 'they,' isn't there?"

"Yes," Eric said. "Yes."

She dumped him three hours later. Left a message on the clunky old answering machine Eric's father kept in the front hall of their house on Parker Hill. On the message, she started out nice, talking about it being her, not him, and how people just drifted apart, they did, and someday she hoped they'd be friends but if he tried any of his crazy shit with her, if he fucking so much as *thought* of doing it, her four brothers would pile out of a car while he was walking Bucky Ave., and they would beat the motherfucking shit out of his crazy fucking ass. Get some help, Eric. Get some serious fucking help. But leave me alone.

He left her alone. She married Paul Giraldi, the electrician, just six months later. Had three kids now.

And Eric was still watching the exit in the back of the same pizza place. Alone.

He thought of using it that morning when the fat guy, Cousin Marv, came over to his table, but he didn't want to make a scene, lose his privileges here again. He'd once been banned for six months in 2005 after the incident with the Sprite and the green peppers and they'd been six of the longest months of his life because Hi-Fi made the best fucking pizza in the history of pizza.

So he stayed where he was as Cousin Marv removed his coat and took the seat across from him.

Cousin Marv said, "I still don't have any Zima."

Eric continued to eat, not sure what the play could be.

Cousin Marv moved the salt and the Parmesan cheese shaker out of their way, stared across the table. "Why don't you like my cousin?"

"He took my dog." Eric slid the Parm shaker back his way.

Cousin Marv said, "I heard you beat it."

"Felt bad about it after." Eric took a small sip of Coke. "That count?"

Cousin Marv looked at him the way a lot of people did— like they could see his thoughts and they found them pitiable.

I'll make you pity yourself someday, Eric thought. *Make you cry and bleed and beg.*

Cousin Marv said, "You even want the dog back?"

Eric said, "I don't know. I don't want your cousin there walking around thinking he's the shit, though. He needs to learn."

Cousin Marv said, "Learn what?"

Eric said, "That he shouldn't have fucked with me. And now you're fucking with me. Think I'm going to put up with that?"

"Relax. I come in peace."

Eric chewed some pizza.

Cousin Marv said, "You ever do time?"

"Time?"

"Yeah," Marv said. "In a prison."

Eric finished his first slice, slapped some crumbs off his hands. "I did time."

"Yeah?" Marv raised his eyebrows. "Where?"

"Broad River."

Marv shook his head. "I don't know it."

"It's in South Carolina."

"Shit," Marv said, "how'd you end up down there?"

Eric shrugged.

"So you did your bid—what, a couple years—and you came back?"

"Yup."

"What was time in South Carolina like?"

Eric lifted his second slice. Looked over it at Cousin Marv. "Like no time at all."

ALL THE TIME TORRES spent looking into the disappearance of Richie Whelan ten years ago yielded pretty much nothing. Kid just up and vanished one night. Left Cousin Marv's Bar, said he'd be back in fifteen, soon as he scored some pot up the block. It had been freezing that night. A lot worse than freezing actually—kind of night made people invest in land they'd never seen in Florida. Six degrees when Richie Whelan left the bar at eleven-forty-five. Torres did a little more digging, found out the wind chill factor that night made that six degrees feel like negative ten. So there's Richie Whelan hustling along the sidewalk in ten-below weather, kind of cold he would have felt burning in his lungs and in the spaces between his lower teeth. No one else on the street that night because only a pothead who'd run out of pot or a cokehead who'd run out of coke would brave that kind of weather for a midnight stroll. Even though the stroll was only three blocks, which was the exact distance between Cousin Marv's Bar and the place where Whelan went to score.

Whelan's alleged dealers that night were two knuckle-heads named Eric Deeds and Tim Brennan. Brennan had given a statement to the police a few days later, said Richie Whelan had never made it to his apartment that night. When asked what his relationship was with Whelan, Tim Brennan had said in his statement, "Sometimes he scored weed off me." Eric Deeds had never given a statement; his name only came up in the statements provided by the friends Richie Whelan had left behind in the bar that night.

So, if Torres accepted that Brennan had no reason to lie, since he'd been reasonably forthcoming about dealing drugs to the missing Richie Whelan, then it was possible to believe Richie Whelan had disappeared within three blocks of Cousin Marv's Bar.

And Torres couldn't shake the suspicion that this little detail carried more weight than any of the prior detectives who'd worked the Whelan disappearance had conferred on it before.

Why? his Loo, Mark Adeline, would have asked (if Torres had been dumb enough to admit he was looking into someone else's cold case).

Because that motherfucker doesn't take Communion, Torres would have said.

In the movie of Torres's life, Mark Adeline would have leaned back in his chair, the mist of wisdom dawning in his eyes, and said, "Huh. You could be onto something there. I'll give you three days."

In reality, Adeline was up his ass to get his fucking Robbery clearance rate up. *Way* up. A new class of recruits was coming out of the Academy. That meant a bunch of patrolmen were about to get bumped up into plainclothes. Robbery, Major Crimes, Homicide, Vice—they'd all be looking for new blood. And the old blood? The ones who chased down other cops' cold cases while their own cases gathered mold and fuzz? They got shipped to the property room or over to the Hackney Carriage Unit, Media Relations, or, worse, the Harbor Unit, enforcing maritime codes in four fucking degrees Fahrenheit. Evandro Torres had case files stacked on his desk and clogging up his hard drive. He had statements he should be taking on a liquor store stickup in Allston, a street rip on Newbury Street, and a smash-n-grab gang working pharmacies all over the city. Plus the stickup of Cousin Marv's. Plus those houses kept getting hit midday in the South End. Plus the delivery trucks down the Seaport kept losing fresh seafood and frozen meat.

Plus, plus, plus. Shit stacked up and then kept stacking higher while the bottom slid out toward a man. Before he knew it he'd been consumed by the stack.

Torres walked to his car, telling himself he was driving to the Seaport to brace that driver he liked for the thefts, the one who was too chummy last time they'd chatted, chewed gum like a squirrel chewed nuts.

But instead he drove over to the electric plant in Southie, the sun coming up just as the night shift was letting out, and had the foreman point out Sean McGrath to him. McGrath was one of Whelan's old buddies and, according to anyone Torres had already chatted up, the leader of the pack of guys who paid tribute to Glory Days once a year on the anniversary of the night he vanished.

Torres introduced himself and started to explain why he'd dropped by, but McGrath held up a hand and called to one of the other guys. "Yo, Jimmy."

"S'up?"

"Where we going?"

"Up the place."

"Place by the deli?"

Jimmy shook his head, lit a cigarette. "Other place."

Sean McGrath said, "Cool."

Jimmy waved and walked off with the other guys.

Sean McGrath turned back to Torres. "So you're asking about the night Richie got in the wind?"

"Yeah. You tell me anything?"

"Nothing to tell. He left the bar. We never saw him again."

"And that's it?"

"That is it," McGrath said. "Believe me, nobody likes it that that's it, but that's it. No one ever saw the guy again.

If there's a Heaven and I make it there, first question out of my mouth—even before 'Who killed JFK?' or, like 'Jesus around?'—is gonna be 'What the fuck happened to my friend Richie Whelan?'"

Torres watched the guy shifting from foot to foot in the morning chill and knew he wouldn't be able to hold him here long. "Your original statement, you said he went to—"

"Score weed, yeah. Guys he usually got it from were that shithead, Tim Brennan, and another guy."

Torres consulted his notebook. "Eric Deeds. That was in your original statement. But let me ask you something."

McGrath blew on his hands. "Sure."

"Bob Saginowski and Cousin Marv? Were they both working that night?"

Sean McGrath stopped blowing on his hands. "You trying to tie them to this?"

Torres said, "I'm just trying to—"

McGrath stepped in close and Torres got that rare whiff of a man who truly shouldn't be fucked with too much. "You know, you come up to me, you say you're with Robbery. But Richie Whelan wasn't robbed. And you got me standing out here, full view of the guys I work with, looking like a snitch. So, I mean, thank you for that."

"Look, Mr. McGrath—"

"Cousin Marv's place? That's my bar." He took another step closer and eye-fucked Torres, breathed heavily through flared nostrils. "Don't fuck with my bar."

He threw Torres a mock salute and walked up the street after his friends.

ERIC DEEDS LOOKED OUT his second-story window as the doorbell rang a second time. He couldn't fucking believe it. That was Bob down there. Bob Saginowski. The Problem. The Dognapper. The Do-Gooder.

Eric heard the squeak of the wheels too late and turned to see his father rolling his wheelchair into the hallway by the intercom.

Eric pointed at him. "Get back in your room."

The old man stared back at him, like a child who hadn't learned how to speak yet. The old man, himself, hadn't been able to speak in nine years and he had a lot of people convinced it made him feeble and retarded and shit, but Eric knew the evil bastard was still in there, still living right behind the skin. Still thinking about ways to get to you, to fuck with you, to make sure the ground below you always felt like quicksand.

The doorbell rang again and the old man ran a finger over the intercom buttons—LISTEN, TALK, and ENTRY.

"I said don't fucking touch anything."

The old man crooked his finger and held it over the ENTRY button.

Eric said, "I'll throw you out this window. Throw that squeaking fucking chair down on top of you while you're fucking lying there."

The old man froze, his eyebrows up.

"I'm serious."

The old man smiled.

"Don't you—"

The old man pressed ENTRY, and held it.

Eric charged across the living room and tackled his father, knocked him the fuck out of that wheelchair. The old man just cackled. Just lay there without his wheelchair, cackling with a soft, distant look in his milk-pale eyes, like he could see into the next world and everyone there was just as full of shit as everyone in this one.

BOB HAD JUST REACHED the sidewalk when he heard the buzzer. He trotted back up the stairs and crossed the porch. He reached for the door just as the buzzer stopped buzzing.

Fuck.

Bob rang the doorbell again. Waited. Rang it again. Waited. He craned his neck off the edge of the front porch, looked up at the second-story window. He went back to the doorbell, pressed it again. After a while, he walked off the porch. He stood on the sidewalk and looked up at the second floor again, wondering if one of the tenants had left the back door open. They often did, or else the landlord didn't pay as much attention if the wood around the lock had rotted over the winter or if termites had gotten to it. But what was Bob going to do—break in? That kind of shit was so far in his rearview mirror it might as well have been the life of a look-alike or a twin he'd never been particularly close to.

He turned to head up the street and Eric Deeds stood right in front of him, staring at him with that fucked-up light in his face, as if he'd been a finalist in a beatification ceremony for people who'd been dropped on their heads as infants. He must have snuck up from the side alley, Bob decided, and now he stood before Bob with an energy coming off him like a power line downed in a storm, hissing and popping in the street.

"You upset my father."

Bob said nothing, but he must have moved his face in a certain way because Eric mocked him with an elaborate up-and-down pantomime of his mouth and eyebrows.

"How many fucking times you gotta ring a doorbell before you decide the people not answering aren't gonna start, Bob? My old man's fucking old. He needs peace and serenity and shit."

"Sorry," Bob said.

Eric liked that. He beamed. "Sorry. That's what you got to say. The old 'sor-ry.'" The smiled died on Eric's face and something so desolate replaced it—the look of a small animal with a broken limb who found himself in a part of the forest he didn't recognize—and then the desolation drowned under a wave of cunning and cold. "Well, you saved me a trip."

"How's that?"

"I was coming by your house later anyway."

Bob said, "I had that feeling, yeah."

"I returned your umbrella."

Bob nodded.

"Coulda taken the dog."

Another nod from Bob.

"But I didn't."

"Why not?" Bob asked.

Eric looked out on the street for a bit as the morning traffic began to thin. "He doesn't fit into my plans anymore."

"Okay," Bob said.

Eric snorted some cold morning air into his nostrils and then hucked louie into the street. "Give me ten thousand."

Bob said, "What?"

"Dollars. By tomorrow morning."

"Who has ten thousand dollars?"

"You could find it."

"How could I poss—?"

"Say, that safe in Cousin Marv's office. That might be a place to start."

Bob shook his head. "Can't be done. It's on a timer—"

"—lock, I know." Eric lit a cigarette. The match caught the wind and the flame found his finger and he shook both until the flame went out. He blew on his finger. "Goes off at two AM and you have ninety seconds to transfer the money from the floor safe or it triggers two silent alarms, neither of which goes off in a police station or a security company. Fancy that." Eric gave him some raised eyebrows again and took a hit off his cigarette. "I'm not greedy, Bob. I just need stake money for something. I don't want everything in the safe, just ten grand. You give me ten grand, I'll disappear."

"This is ridiculous."

"So, it's ridiculous."

"You don't just walk into someone's life and—"

"That *is* life—someone like me coming along when you're not looking and you're not ready. I'm a hundred seventy pounds' worth of End Times, Bob."

Bob said, "There's gotta be another way."

Eric Deeds's eyebrows went up and down again. "You're racing through all your options, but they're options for normal people in normal circumstances. I'm not offering those things. I need my ten grand. You get it tonight, I'll pick it up tomorrow morning. For all you know, I'm betting it on the Super Bowl, got me a sure thing. You just be at your house tomorrow morning at nine sharp with ten grand. If you don't, I'll jump up and down on that bitch-whore Nadia's head until her neck snaps and there's no face left. Then I'll beat the dog's head in with a rock. Look in my eyes and tell me which part I'm lying about, Bob."

Bob met his eyes. Not for the first time in his life, and not for the last, he had to swallow against the nausea that roiled his stomach in the face of cruelty. It was all he could do not to vomit in Eric's face.

"What is *wrong* with you?" Bob said.

Eric held out his hands. "Pretty much everything. I'm severely fucked in the ol' squash, Bob. And you took my dog."

"You tried to kill it."

"Nah." Eric shook his head like he believed it. "You heard what I did to Richie Whelan, right?"

Bob nodded.

Eric said, "Piece of shit, that kid. Caught him trying to tap my girl's shit so bye-bye, Richie. Reason I bring him up, Bob? I had me a partner on the Richie thing. I still have him. So you think of doing anything to me? Then you'll spend the rest of your limited days of freedom wondering when my partner's going to come for his or drop a dime to Five-O." Eric flicked his cigarette into the street. "Anything else, Bob?"

Bob didn't say a fucking word.

"See you in the morning." Eric left him on the sidewalk and headed back into his house.

"WHO *IS* HE?" BOB asked Nadia as they walked Rocco through the park.

"Who is he?" Nadia said. "Or 'Who is he to me?'"

The river had frozen again last night but the ice was already coming apart in a series of cracks and moans. Rocco kept trying to place a paw over the edge of the bank, and Bob kept snapping him back.

"To you, then."

"I told you. We dated for a while." She shrugged her narrow shoulders. "He's a guy who grew up on my street. He goes in and out of prison. Hospitals too. People say he killed Richie Whelan back in oh-four."

"People say it, or he says it?"

Another shrug. "'Mounts to the same thing."

"Why'd he kill Richie Whelan?"

"I heard he was trying to impress some hard guys down on Stoughton Street."

"Leo's crew."

She looked at him, her face a white moon under her black hoodie. "That's the rumor."

"So he's a bad guy."

"Everyone's bad."

"No," Bob said, "they're not. Most people are okay."

"Yeah?" A smile of disbelief.

"Yeah. They just, I dunno, make a lotta messes and then they make more messes trying to clean those first messes up and after a while that's your life."

She sniffled and chuckled at the same time. "That's it, uh?"

"That's it sometimes." He looked at the dark red cord around her neck.

She noticed. "How come you've never asked?"

"I told you—I didn't think it would be polite."

She smiled that heartbreaker of hers. "Polite? Who has those kind of manners anymore?"

"No one," he admitted. It felt a bit tragic, that admission, as if too many things that actually should matter in the world had lost their place in line. You'd wake up one day and it would all be gone, like 8-tracks or newspapers. "Was it Eric Deeds?"

She shook her head. Then she nodded. Then she shook her head again. "He did something to me during one of his, I dunno—the shrinks call it 'manic periods.' I didn't take it well. I had a lot of other shit coming down on my head at the same time, it wasn't just him—"

"Yes, it was."

"—but he was definitely the last straw."

"You cut your own throat?"

She loosed a series of short, quick nods. "I was pretty high."

Bob said, "You did that to yourself?"

Nadia said, "With a box cutter. One of those—"

"Oh, God. No, I know what they are." Bob repeated it: "You did that to yourself?"

Nadia stared back at him. "I was a different person. I didn't, you know, like myself at all?"

Bob said, "You like yourself now?"

Nadia shrugged.

Bob said nothing. He knew if he spoke he'd kill something that deserved life.

After a while, Nadia looked at Bob, her eyes gleaming, and shrugged again.

They walked for a bit.

"Did you ever see him with Rocco?"

"Huh?"

"Did you? I mean, he lived on your block."

"No, I don't think."

"You don't *think*?"

She took a step back. "Who are you right now, Bob? 'Cause you're not yourself."

"I am," he assured her. He softened his voice. "Did you ever see Eric Deeds with Rocco?"

Another series of quick nods, like a bird bobbing for water.

"So you knew it was his dog."

Those nods kept coming, short and fast.

"That he threw in the trash." Bob let loose a low sigh. "Right."

They crossed a small wooden bridge over a patch of still-frozen river, the ice gone light blue and thin, but holding.

"So he says he just wants ten thousand?" she said eventually.

Bob nodded.

"But if you lose that ten thousand?"

"Someone will pay."

"You?"

"And Marv. Both of us. Place already got held up once."

"Will they kill you?"

"It depends. A group of them will get together, the Chechens, the 'Talians, the Micks. Five or six fat guys having coffee in some parking lot, and they'll make a decision. For ten grand on top of the five we lost in the robbery? It wouldn't look good." He looked up at the bald sky. "I mean, I could scratch together ten on my own. I've been saving up."

"For what? What does Bob Saginowski save up for?"

Bob said nothing until she let it go.

"So if you can come up with the ten . . ." she said.

"It wouldn't be enough."

"But that's what he's asking for."

"Sure," Bob said, "but that's not what he *wants*. A starving man sees a bag of potato chips, right? And it's the only bag for, who knows, ever. He eats three-four chips every four hours, he can make that bag last five days? But do you think he's going to do that?"

"He'll eat the whole bag."

Bob nodded.

"What're you going to do?"

Rocco made another try for the river's edge and Bob pulled him back. He bent and tapped the dog's nose with his index finger. "No. Okay? No." He looked up at Nadia. "I have no idea."

CHAPTER 13

Remember Me

ON CAUSEWAY STREET, THE Bruins game was letting out into the rain. Cousin Marv had to pull to the curb with the cops screaming at everyone to keep moving and the crowds jostling past and rocking the chassis of the Honda, the cabs honking their horns, the rain sluicing down the windshield like bouillabaisse. Marv was just about to pull away, loop the block, which, in this traffic, would take half a fucking hour, when Fitz materialized out of the crowd and stopped a few feet short of the door, staring in at Marv with a pale sunken face under a dark vinyl hood.

Marv rolled down the passenger window of the weary, faded-gold Honda. "Come on."

Fitz stayed where he was.

"What," Marv said, "you think I got the trunk lined with plastic?" He popped the trunk. "Go see for yourself."

Fitz flicked his eyes that way but didn't move. "I ain't getting in with you."

"Seriously? We gotta talk."

"They got my brother," Fitz shouted through the rain.

Marv nodded, reasonable. "I'm not sure the cop at the intersection heard that. Or that one right behind you there, Fitzy."

Fitz looked behind him at the young cop working crowd control a few feet away. Oblivious for now. But that could change.

Marv said, "This is retarded. About two thousand people, including cops, have seen us talking by this car. It's fucking freezing. Get in."

Fitz took a step toward the car, then stopped. He called, "Hey, Officer! Officer!"

The young cop turned, looked at him.

Fitz pointed at his own chest and then at the Honda. "You remember me. Okay?"

The cop pointed. "Move that car!"

Fitz gave him a thumbs-up. "My name's Fitz."

The cop shouted, "Move!"

Fitz opened the door but Marv stopped him. "Shut the trunk, will ya?"

Fitz ran back in the rain, shut the trunk. He climbed in

the car. Cousin Marv rolled up the window and they pulled away from the curb.

Soon as they did, Fitz lifted his jacket, flashed the .38 snub in his waistband. "Don't fuck with me. Don't you fucking dare. Hear? You hear?"

Cousin Marv said, "Your mommy pack that gun in your lunch box for you? Christ, packing heat like you're in a fucking Red State, scared the spics are coming for your job and the niggers are coming for your wife. That it?"

Fitz said, "Last time anyone saw my brother alive, he got in a car with a guy."

Cousin Marv said, "Your brother probably had a gun too."

"Fuck you, Marv."

"Listen, I'm sorry, Fitz, I am. But you know me—I ain't no shooter, man. I'm just a scared shitless bar manager. I want a do-over for this whole fucking year." Marv looked out the window as they rode the bumper-to-bumper traffic toward Storrow Drive. He glanced at the gun again. "Make your dick bigger if you held that on me all sideways-gangsta-style and shit?"

Fitz said, "You're an asshole, Marv."

Marv chuckled. "Tell me something I don't know."

The traffic thinned a bit once they got onto Storrow and headed west.

"We're gonna die," Fitz said. "That sink in yet for you?"

Cousin Marv said, "This is a risk-versus-reward thing now, Fitzy. We already took the risk, and, yeah, it doesn't seem to be working out well."

Fitz lit a cigarette. "But?"

"But I know where the Super Bowl drop's going to be to-morrow. The drop of drops. You want to hit 'em back for your brother? Hit 'em for a million."

Fitz said, "Fucking suicide."

Cousin Marv said, "This point, we're both waiting around to die anyway. I'd rather go on the run with a chest of money than hit the road broke."

Fitz gave it some thought, his right knee tap-tap-tapping against the underside of the glove box. "I'm not doing another one, man."

Cousin Marv said, "Your choice. I won't beg your help carving up a seven-figure payday."

"I never saw my cut of a lousy five grand we took the first time."

Cousin Marv said, "But you had it."

Fitz said, "Bri had it."

The traffic had thinned considerably as they drove past Harvard Stadium, first football stadium in the country and yet one more building that seemed to mock Marv, one more place he'd have been laughed out of if he'd ever tried to walk in. That's what this city did—it placed its history in your face at every turn so you could feel less significant in its shadow.

Cousin Marv turned west with the river and now there was no one on the road. "I'll square it with you then."

Fitz said, "What?"

"Seriously. But I'm buying something with it—first, you

don't say a fucking thing about what I told you. And second, you got a place I can hole up a couple days?"

Fitz said, "You're on the street?"

A metallic slapping sound found them now, and Marv looked in the rearview, saw the trunk quivering up and down in the rain.

"Fucking trunk. You didn't close it."

Fitz said, "I closed it."

"Not well."

The trunk continued to flap up and down.

Cousin Marv said, "And no, I'm not on the street, but everyone knows where I live. You, on the other hand, *I* don't even know where you live."

The trunk swung down against the car and then bounced back up again.

Fitz said, "I closed that thing."

"So you say."

"Fuck it, pull over. Let me get it."

Marv pulled into one of the parking lots along the Charles rumored to be a hookup place for queers married to women in their daily lives. The only other car in the entire lot was an old American shitbox that looked like it had been there a week, old snow on the grille fighting a losing battle against the rain. It was Saturday, Marv remembered, which meant the queers were probably home with the wives and kids, pretending not to like cock and Kate Hudson movies. Place was desolate.

Marv said to Fitz, "Can I shack up with you or not? Just tonight and maybe, okay, tomorrow night?"

He pulled the car to a stop.

Fitz said, "Not with me, but I know a place."

Cousin Marv said, "It got cable?"

Fitz, getting out of the car, said, "Motherfucker, what?"

He ran to the back of the car and slammed down the trunk with one hand. He came back to the passenger door and his head snapped as the trunk opened again.

Marv watched Fitz's face tighten in rage. He ran to the back again, grabbed the top of the trunk with both hands, and slammed it down so hard the entire car moved, Marv and all.

Then the brake lights that were bathing his face red vanished. He locked eyes with Marv in the rearview and in that last second he saw the play. The hate that found his eyes seemed less directed at Marv and more at his own dumb ass.

The Honda rocked on all fours when Marv slammed it into reverse and drove over Fitz. He heard a yelp, just one, and even that was distant, and it was easy to imagine that what was scraping the underside of the car was a bag of potatoes or a really fucking huge holiday turkey.

"Fuck, man." Marv heard his own voice in the rain. "Fuck, fuck, fuck."

And then he drove forward over Fitz. Hit the brakes. Shifted into reverse. Did it all over again.

After a few more times, he left the body and drove over to

his own car. He didn't need to wipe down the Honda—the best thing about winter was that everyone wore gloves. You could keep them on going to bed at night and no one got suspicious, just asked where they could get themselves a pair.

When he got out of the Honda, he looked across the parking lot to where Fitz's body lay. You could barely see it from here. From this distance, it could have been a pile of wet leaves or old snow eroding under the steady rain. Hell, from here, what he thought was Fitz's body could be just a trick of light and shadow.

I am, Marv realized in that moment, as dangerous as the most dangerous man alive right now. I have taken life.

It wasn't an unpleasant thought.

Marv got in his car and drove off. For the second time that week, he reminded himself that he needed new wipers.

BOB DESCENDED THE CELLAR stairs with Rocco in his arms. The main room was empty and spotless, the stone floor and stone walls painted white. Against the wall, opposite the base of the stairs, stood a black oil tank. Bob walked past it the way he always did—quickly and with his head down—and carried Rocco to one corner of the cellar where his father had installed a sink many years ago. Beside the sink was some shelving with old tools and boots and paint cans on it. Above the sink was a cupboard. Bob put Rocco down in the sink.

He opened the cupboard. It was filled with spray paint

cans and jars of screws and nails, a few cans of paint remover. He pulled down a Chock full o'Nuts coffee can and placed it beside the sink. With Rocco staring at him, he removed a plastic Baggie filled with small bolts. He then pulled out a roll of hundred-dollar bills. There were other rolls in there as well. Five more of them. Bob had always figured that some-day, when he died, someone would come across this can while they were cleaning out the house and pocket the money, swear themselves to secrecy. But, of course, that never worked, and word would leak out and become urban legend—the guy who found over fifty thousand dollars in a coffee can in the cellar of a lonely old man's house. The idea had always pleased Bob for some reason. He put the roll in his pocket and the plastic Baggie of screws back on top and closed the coffee can. He placed it back in the cupboard, then closed and locked the cupboard.

Bob counted the money with the speed only bartenders and casino dealers had. All there. Ten grand. He waved the sheaf of money in front of Rocco, fanning his face with it.

Bob said, "You worth it?"

The puppy looked back at him, head cocked.

"I don't know," Bob said. "It's a lot of money."

Rocco put his front paws on the edge of the sink and nib-bled Bob's wrist with those sharp, spiky puppy teeth.

Bob scooped him up with his free hand and pressed their faces together. "I'm kidding, I'm kidding. You're worth it."

He and Rocco and walked out of the back room. This

time, when he reached the black oil tank, he stopped. He stood in front of it with his head down, and then he looked up. For the first time in years, he stared directly at it. The pipes that had once been coupled to it—a receiving pipe to receive oil via the outside wall and a heating pipe to heat the house—had long since been removed and the holes sealed.

Inside, instead of oil, were lye, rock salt, and, by this point, bones. Just bones.

In his darkest days, when he'd nearly lost faith and hope, when he'd danced with despair and wrestled her in his sheets at night, he'd felt pieces of his mind detach, like the heat shields of starships that had glanced off an asteroid. He imagined those pieces of him spinning off into space, never to return.

But they did come back. And most of the rest of him came back too.

He climbed the stairs with Rocco and looked back down at the oil tank one last time.

Bless me, Father . . .

He shut off the light. He could hear his and the dog's breathing in the dark.

. . . for I have sinned.

CHAPTER 14

Other Selves

SUPER BOWL SUNDAY.

More money bet than would be bet the rest of the year on the NCAA Final Four, the Kentucky Derby, the NBA Championship Series, the Stanley Cup, and the World Series combined. If paper money hadn't been invented yet, they would have created it just to handle the weight and volume of today's wagers. Little old ladies who couldn't tell pigskin from pigs' feet had a feeling about the Seahawks; Guatemalan illegals who carried the clean-up buckets on construction sites thought Manning was the closest thing to the second coming of our Lord and savior. *Everyone* bet, everyone watched.

As he waited for Eric Deeds to drop by his house, Bob

indulged himself in a second cup of coffee because he knew the longest day of his year awaited. Rocco lay on the floor at his feet, chewing on a rope chew toy. Bob had placed the ten thousand dollars in the center of the table. He arranged the chairs just so. He placed his chair next to the counter drawer with his old man's .32 in there, just in case. Just in case. He opened the drawer, looked inside. He moved the drawer back and forth for the twentieth time, made sure it was loose. He sat and tried to read the *Globe* and then the *Herald*. He placed his hands on the tabletop.

Eric never showed.

Bob didn't know what to make of it, but it sat badly in the pit of his stomach, sat there like a fiddler crab, scratching its way from side to side, scuttling in fear.

Bob waited some more and then waited some more past that, but finally it was too late to do any more waiting around.

He left the gun where it was. He wrapped the money in a plastic Shaw's bag and put it in the pocket of his coat and got the leash.

In his car, he'd placed the dog crate, folded up, in the backseat along with a blanket, some chew toys, a bowl, and dog food. He'd placed a towel on the front passenger seat and he lifted Rocco onto it and they set off into their day.

AT COUSIN MARV'S HOUSE, Bob made sure the car was locked and the alarm on before he left Rocco snoozing inside and knocked on the door to Marv's.

Dottie was shrugging into her coat when she let him in. Bob stood in the foyer with her, kicking the salt off the bottom of his boots.

"Where you heading?" he asked Dottie.

"Work. Time-and-a-half on weekends, Bobby."

"I thought you took the early retirement."

Dottie said, "To what? I'll do another year or two, hope the phlebitis don't get too bad, see where I'm at. Get my baby brother to eat something. I left a plate in the fridge."

Bob said, "Okay."

Dottie said, "He just has to microwave it a minute and a half. Have a good day."

Bob said, "You too, Dottie."

Dottie screamed back into the house at the top of her lungs, "I'm off to work!"

Cousin Marv said, "Good day, Dot'."

Dottie screamed, "You too! Eat something!"

Dottie and Bob exchanged kisses on the cheek and then she was gone.

Bob walked down the hall to the den, found Cousin Marv sitting in a Barcalounger staring at the TV. A pregame show on there now, Dan Marino and Bill Cowher doing X's and O's on a board in their four-thousand-dollar suits.

Bob said, "Dottie says you need to eat."

Cousin Marv said, "Dottie says a lot of things. At tip-top fucking volume too."

Bob said, "She might have to, get you to listen."

Cousin Marv said, "And that means what exactly? 'Cause I'm slow."

Bob said, "Biggest day of the year today and I can't get you on the phone."

Cousin Marv said, "I'm not coming in. Call BarTemps."

"'Call BarTemps.'" Bob said, "Jesus. I already did. It's Super Bowl."

Cousin Marv said, "So why do you need me?"

Bob sat in the other Barcalounger. As a kid, he'd liked this room, but as the years passed and it stayed exactly the same except for a new TV every five years, it felt like heartbreak to him. Like a calendar page no one bothered to turn anymore.

Bob said, "I don't need you. But you're blowing off the biggest tip day of the year?"

"Oh, I work for tips now." Cousin Marv stared at the screen, wearing a ridiculous red, white, and blue Patriots jersey and matching sweats. "You ever see the name on the bar? It's mine. Know why? 'Cause I owned it once."

Bob said, "You nurse that loss like it was your one good lung."

Cousin Marv whipped his head around, glared at him, "You've been getting awful fucking fresh since you picked up that dog you confuse with a kid."

Bob said, "You can't redo it. They pressed, you blinked, it's over. It's been over."

Cousin Marv reached for the lever on the side of the chair. "I'm not the one wasted my whole life waiting for it to start."

Bob said, "That's what I did?"

Cousin Marv pulled the lever, let his feet down to the floor. "Yeah. So fuck you and your eeney-weeny fucking dreams. I was feared once. That fucking barstool where you let that old biddy sit? That was my barstool. And no one sat there because it was Cousin Marv's seat. That meant something."

"No, Marv," Bob said, "it was just a chair."

Cousin Marv's eyes returned to the TV. Boomer and JB on there now, yucking it up.

Bob leaned in, spoke very softly but very clearly. "You doing something desperate again? Marv, listen to me. Hear me. Are you doing something we won't be able to clean up this time?"

Cousin Marv leaned back in the chair until the footrest rose under his legs again. He wouldn't look at Bob. He lit a cigarette. "Get the fuck out. Really."

IN THE BACK OF the bar, Bob set up the crate, laid the blanket in it, and tossed in the chew toys, but he let Rocco run around for a while. Worst that would happen is the puppy would take a shit somewhere, and they had cleaning supplies and a hose for that.

He went behind the bar. He pulled the bag with the ten thousand dollars from his coat and placed it on the shelf beside the same 9mm semiautomatic Cousin Marv had wisely opted not to use during the robbery. He pushed the money and the handgun back into the shadows of the shelf using a shrink-wrapped deck of coasters. He added another deck in front of the first one.

He watched Rocco run around and sniff everywhere—time of his life—and without Marv in here like he should be, on this of all days, Bob saw every inch of the world as quicksand. There was no firm purchase. There was no safe place on which to place his feet.

How had it come to this?

You let the world in, Bobby, a voice that sounded an awful lot like his mother's said. You let this sin-dripping world in. And the only thing under its cloak is darkness.

But, Mother?

Yes, Bobby.

It was time. I can't just live for the other world. I need to live in this one now.

So say the fallen. So they've said since time began.

THEY BROUGHT AN EMACIATED Tim Brennan into the visiting room at Concord Prison and sat him across from Torres.

Torres said, "Mr. Brennan, thanks for meeting me."

Tim Brennan said, "Game'll be starting soon. I don't want to lose my seat."

Torres said, "No worries. I'll be in and out of here in no time. What can you tell me about Richie Whelan? Anything?"

Brennan launched into a sudden and violent coughing fit.

It sounded like he was drowning in phlegm and razors. When he finally got a handle on it, he spent another minute clutching his chest and wheezing. When he looked across the table at Torres again, he did so with the eyes of a man who'd already glimpsed the other side.

Tim Brennan said, "I tell my kids I got a stomach virus. Me and the wife don't know how to tell 'em I got AIDS in here. So we go with a story until they're ready for the truth. Which do you want?"

"Excuse me?" Torres said.

"You want the story about the night Richie Whelan died? Or you want the truth?"

Torres's scalp itched the way it did whenever a case was about to break wide open, but he kept his face a blank, his eyes pleasant and accepting. "Whichever one you're giving today, Tim."

ERIC DEEDS LET HIMSELF into Nadia's house with a credit card and the kind of tiny screwdriver usually used on eyeglass arms. It took fourteen tries, but there was no one out on the street so no one saw him up on the porch in the first place. Everyone had done their shopping—got their beer and chips, their artichoke dip and onion dip and salsa, their chicken wings and spare ribs, their popcorn—and now they were hunkered down, waiting for kickoff, which was still over three hours away but, hey, who gave a shit about time when you'd started drinking at noon?

Once he was inside, he paused and listened to the house as he pocketed the screwdriver and the credit card, which had gotten pretty banged up in the process. But, fuck it, they'd canceled it on Eric months ago anyway.

Eric walked down the hall and pushed open the doors on the living room, the dining room, the bathroom, and the kitchen.

Then he went upstairs to Nadia's bedroom.

He went right to the closet. He looked through her clothes. He sniffed a few. And they smelled like her—a faint mix of orange, cherry, and chocolate. That's what Nadia smelled like.

Eric sat on the bed.

Eric stood in front of her mirror, finger-combed his hair.

Eric pulled back the covers on her bed. He removed his shoes. He curled on the bed in a fetal position, pulled the covers over himself. He closed his eyes. He smiled. He felt the smile find his blood and ride it through his entire body. He felt safe. Like he'd crawled back into the womb. Like he could breathe water again.

AFTER HIS ASSHOLE FUCKING cousin left, Marv got to work at the kitchen table. He lay several green plastic trash bags on it and carefully taped them together with electrical tape. He got a beer from the fridge and drained half of it, staring at the bags on the table. As if there was any turning back.

There was no turning back. There never had been.

Sucked in some ways because Marv realized, standing in his shitty kitchen, how much he'd miss it. Miss his sister, miss this house, even miss the bar and his cousin Bob.

But there was no fixing it. Life was regret, after all. And some regrets—those you indulged on a beach in Thailand, for example, over those you indulged in a New England graveyard—were more easily swallowed than others.

To Thailand. He raised his beer to the empty kitchen and then he drained it.

ERIC SAT ON THE sofa in Nadia's living room. He drank a Coke he'd found in her fridge—well, *their* fridge, it would be their fridge soon enough—and stared at the faded wallpaper that had probably been here since before Nadia was born. That would be the first thing that had to go, that old 1970s wallpaper. Wasn't the '70s no more, wasn't even the twentieth century. It was a new day.

When he finished the Coke, he took it into the kitchen and made a sandwich from some deli meat he found in the fridge.

He heard a noise and looked up at the doorway and there she stood. Nadia. Looking at him. Curious, of course, but not afraid. A kindness in her eyes. A warm grace.

Eric said, "Oh, hey. How you doing? Been a while. Come on in, take a seat."

She stayed where she was.

Eric said, "Yeah, no, sit. Sit. I want to tell you some things. I got some plans. Yeah. Plans. Right? Whole new life waiting out there for the, for the, for the bold."

Eric shook his head. He didn't like that delivery. He lowered his head, looked up at the doorway again. It was empty. He stared at it until she materialized, and she was no longer wearing jeans and a faded plaid work shirt. She was wearing a dark dress with very small polka dots, and her skin . . . her skin shined.

"Oh, *hey*," Eric said happily. "How's it going, girl? Come on in. Take a—"

He stopped at the sound of a key turning the lock on the front door. The door opened. Closed. He heard a handbag being hung on a hook. Keys dropped on a table. The thud of boots being kicked off.

He adjusted himself in the chair to look comfortable, casual. He lightly slapped the bread crumbs off his hands and touched his hair to make sure it was in place.

Nadia entered. The real Nadia. Hoodie and T-shirt over camo cargo pants. Eric would have preferred a slightly less dykey getup but he'd talk it out with her.

She saw him and opened her mouth.

"Don't scream," he said.

THINGS BEGAN TO REALLY pick up about four hours before the game. Which was good timing because that's when the

BarTemps crew showed up. They were already getting to it, putting on their aprons, stacking glasses, when Bob met with their supervisor, a red-haired guy with one of those moon faces that never aged. He said to Bob, "They're contracted till midnight. Anything later'n that, we gotta charge. I gave you two barbacks. They do all the lifting, trash removal, all the ice runs. You ask one of the 'tenders to do it? They'll start quoting you union bylaws like it's the Book of Ezekiel."

He handed Bob the clipboard and Bob signed off.

By the time he walked back into the bar, the first bagman was coming through the door. He dropped a newspaper on the bar, a manila envelope peeking out between the folds, and Bob swiped it off the bar, dropped the envelope down the chute. When he turned around the bagman was gone. All work, no play. That kind of night.

COUSIN MARV WALKED OUT of his house to his car. He popped the trunk. He took the taped-together trash bags and lay them across the inside of the empty trunk. He used more electrical tape to seal all the edges against the sides.

He walked back into the house, grabbed the quilt from the mudroom. He lay the quilt over the plastic. He studied his handiwork for a few seconds. Then he shut the trunk, put the suitcase behind the driver's seat, and closed the door.

He went back inside to print out the plane tickets.

THIS TIME WHEN TORRES pulled up beside Romsey's un-marked at Pen' Park, she was alone. It got him wondering if they could go all old school in the backseat, pretend they were at the drive-in that used to be here, pretend they were stupid kids and a whole lifetime—two of them—lay waiting to unfurl before them, as yet smooth and untouched by the pockmarks of poor decisions and the divots of habitual fail-ures, large and small.

He and Romsey had slipped up again last week. Alcohol had, of course, been a factor. After, she'd said, "Is this all I am?"

"To me? No, chica, you're—"

"To me," she said. "Is this all I am to me?"

He didn't know what the fuck that meant but he knew it wasn't good, so he'd laid low until she called him this morn-ing, told him to get his ass over to Pen' Park.

He'd composed a speech on the way over, in case she got that look in her eyes after they did it, that hopeless, self-hating look, the one looking down the rabbit hole in the center of herself.

"Baby," he'd say, "we're each other's true selves. That's why we can't quit each other. We look at each other and we don't judge. We don't condemn. We just accept."

It had sounded better when he came up with it the other night at the bar, sitting alone, doodling. But he knew, if he was looking in her eyes, feeding off them, he'd believe it in that moment, believe every word. And he'd sell it.

When he opened the door and slid into the passenger side, he noticed she was nicely dressed up—dark green silk dress, black pumps, black coat looked to be cashmere.

Torres said, "You're looking fucking yummy. Shit."

Romsey rolled her eyes. She reached down between the seats, came back with a file, and tossed it on his lap. "Eric Deeds's psych file. You've got three minutes to read it and better not be no grease on those fingers."

Torres held up his hands, wiggled the fingers. Romsey pulled a compact out of her purse, started applying blush to her face, eyes on the visor mirror.

"Better get reading," she said.

Torres opened the file and noticed the name stamped up top—DEEDS, ERIC—and started skimming through it.

Romsey pulled out some lipstick, went to apply it.

Torres, eyes on the file, said to her, "Don't. Chica, you got lips redder than a Jamaican sunset and thicker than a Burmese python. Don't fuck with flawless."

She looked at him. She seemed touched. Then she applied the lipstick anyway. Torres sighed.

Torres said, "Like using house paint on a Ferrari. Who you going out with anyway?"

"A guy."

He turned a page. "A guy. What guy?"

"Special guy," she said and something in her tone made him look up. He noticed for the first time that in addition to looking hot, she looked healthy. Like she was lit from within.

It was a light that filled the car so completely he couldn't understand how he'd missed it.

"Where'd you meet this special guy?"

She pointed at the file. "Get reading. Clock's ticking."

He did.

"I'm serious," he said. "This special guy. He . . ."

His voice trailed off. He scanned back up the page to the list of Deeds's incarcerations and institutionalizations. He thought maybe he'd read a date wrong. He flipped a page, then another.

He said, "Well, I'll be damned."

"Like you fucking weren't already." She indicated the file. "It help?"

"I don't know," he said. "It sure answered one hell of a question."

"That's good, right?"

He shrugged. "Answered one question, yeah, but opened a big can of other ones." Torres closed the file, his blood the cold of the Atlantic. "I need a drink. Buy you one?"

Romsey gave him a look of disbelief. She gestured at her clothes, her hair, her makeup. "Other plans, Evandro."

Torres said, "Rain check then."

And Detective Lisa Romsey gave him a slow, sad shake of her head. "This special guy? I've known him most of my life," she said. "He's been my friend, you know? A long time. He moved away for years but we stayed in touch. His marriage didn't work out either, he moved back. One day, a couple weeks back? I'm having coffee with him and I realize that when he looks at me, he sees me."

"I see you."

She shook her head. "You only see the part of me that looks like you. Which ain't the best part, Evandro. Sorry. But my friend—my *friend*? He looks at me and sees the best me." She smacked her lips. "And just like that?" She shrugged. "Love."

He looked at her for a bit. There it was, without warning—the end of them. Whatever "them" was. It was no longer. He handed her the file.

He got out of her unmarked and she drove off before he even reached his car.

CHAPTER 15

Closing Time

THE BAGMEN CAME AND went. In and out, all night long. Bob dropped so much money through the slot, he knew he'd hear the sound of it in his dreams for days.

Three deep at the bar through the whole game; he looked through a sudden gap in the crowd just after halftime and saw Eric Deeds sitting at the wobbly table under the Narragansett mirror. He had one arm stretched across the table and Bob followed it, saw that it connected with someone's arm. Bob had to move down the bar to get a better angle around a clump of drunks, and he immediately wished he hadn't. Wished he'd never come to work. Wished he'd never gotten up any day since Christmas. Wished he could turn back the clock on his whole life, just reset it to the day before he walked down that block and found Rocco outside her house.

Nadia's house.

It was Nadia's arm Deeds touched, Nadia's face staring back at Eric, unreadable.

Bob, filling a glass with ice, felt like he was shoveling the cubes into his own chest, pouring them into his stomach and against the base of his spine. What did he know about Nadia, after all? He knew that he'd found a near-dead dog in the trash outside her house. He knew that she had a history—of some kind—with Eric Deeds and that Eric Deeds only came into his life after Bob had met her. He knew that her middle name, thus far, could be Lies of Omission. Maybe that scar on her throat hadn't come from her own hand, maybe it had come from the last guy she'd scammed.

When he was twenty-eight, Bob had come into his mother's bedroom to wake her for Sunday mass. He'd given her a shake and she hadn't batted at his hand as she normally did. So he rolled her toward him and her face was scrunched tight, her eyes too, and her skin was curbstone gray. Sometime in the night, after *The Commish* and the *Eleven O'Clock News,* she'd gone to bed and woke to God's fist clenched around her heart. Probably hadn't been enough air left in her lungs to cry out. Alone in the dark, clutching the sheets, the fist clenching, her face clenching, her eyes scrunching, the terrible knowledge dawning that, even for you and right now, it all ends.

Standing over her that morning, imagining the last tick of

her heart, the last lonely wish her brain had been able to form, Bob felt a loss unlike any he expected to know again.

Until tonight. Until now. Until he knew what that look on Nadia's face meant.

MIDWAY THROUGH THE THIRD quarter, Bob came down the bar to a group of guys. One of them had his back to him and there was something really familiar about the back of his head, Bob about to put his finger on it when Rardy turned and gave him a big smile.

Rardy said, "How you doing there, Bobby boy?"

"We, we," Bob said, "we were worried about you."

Rardy gave that comical scowl. "You, you, you were? We'll have seven beers and seven shots of Cuervo by the way."

Bob said, "We thought you were dead."

Rardy said, "Why would I be dead? I just didn't feel like working in a place almost got me killed. Tell Marv he'll be hearing from my lawyer."

Bob saw Eric Deeds working his way through the crowd toward the other side of the bar, and it put something in the center of Bob, something heartless. He said to Rardy, "Maybe I'll tell Chovka about your complaints. Pass that up the ladder. Whatta ya think? Good idea?"

Rardy laughed bitterly at that, trying for contempt but not getting anywhere close. He shook his head several times, like Bob just didn't get something, didn't get anything.

"Give us the beers and the shots."

Bob leaned into the bar, got real close, close enough to smell the tequila on Rardy's breath. "You want a drink? Flag down a bartender who doesn't know you're a bag of shit."

Rardy blinked but Bob was already walking away.

He crossed behind a couple of the BarTemps and stood at the other corner and watched Eric Deeds come.

When he reached him, Eric said, "Stoli rocks, my man. House Chard' for the lady."

Bob made the drink. "Didn't see you this morning."

"No? Well . . ."

"So, you don't want the money."

Eric said, "You bring it with you?"

"Bring what?"

"You did. You're that type."

Bob said, "What type?"

"Type would bring the money with him."

Bob delivered the Stoli, poured a glass of Chardonnay. "Why's she here?"

"She's my girl. Always-n-f'eva and shit."

Bob slid the wineglass in front of Eric. He leaned into the bar. Eric leaned in to meet him.

Bob said, "You give me that piece of paper and you leave with the money."

"What piece of paper?"

"The microchip piece. You sign over that and the license to me."

"Why would I do that?"

Bob said, "Because I'm paying you. Isn't that the deal?"

Eric said, "That's *a* deal."

Eric's cell phone rang. He looked at it, held up a finger to Bob. He took the drinks and walked back into the crowd.

ADD PEYTON MANNING TO the list of people who had fucked Cousin Marv up the ass in his life. Motherfucker went out there with his billion-dollar arm and his billion-dollar contract and wet-shit all over the field against the Seahawks defense. There were two kinds of Bronco-busting going on right now—what Seattle was doing to Denver and what Denver was doing to every bettor in the country who'd put their faith in them. Marv, one of those bettors—because what was the point of continuing to abstain from bad habits if you were insane enough to rip off the Chechen Mafia for a few million dollars?—was gonna lose fifty grand on this fucking game. Not that he was gonna stick around to pay the debt. And if that pissed off Leo Coogan and his Upham Corner boys, well, they could just get in line. Take a fucking number.

From the kitchen phone, Marv called the Deeds kid to see when he planned to head over to the bar and was shocked and sickened to hear that he was already there and had been for an hour.

"The fuck are you doing?" he said.

"Where else am I going to be?" Deeds said.

"Home. So nobody gets a good look at you until you, you know, rob the fucking place."

"No one ever notices me," Eric said, "so don't worry about it."

"I just don't get it," Marv said.

"Get what?"

"This was so simple—you show up at the designated time, do the thing, and leave. Why can't anyone just stick to a fucking plan in this world anymore? Your generation, you all pack your assholes with ADD before you leave the house every morning?"

Marv went to the fridge for another beer.

Deeds said, "Don't worry about it. I'm in his head."

"Whose head?"

"Bob's."

"If you were in that guy's head you'd be screaming, and you're not screaming." Marv cracked the beer. He softened his voice a bit. Better to have a chilled-out partner than one who thought you were pissed at him. "Look, I know what he seems like, but I shit you not, do not fuck with that man. Just leave him alone and don't call attention to yourself."

"Oh," Eric said, "so what am I supposed to do for the next couple hours?"

"You're in a bar. Don't drink too fucking much, stay frosty, and I'll see you at two in the alley. That sound like a plan?"

Eric's laughter came through the receiver strained and girlish at the same time, like he was laughing at a joke no one else could hear and no one else would get if they could.

"Sounds like *a* plan," he said and hung up.

Marv stared at his phone. Kids these days. It was like on that day in school when they taught personal responsibility, this entire fucking generation had banged in sick.

ONCE THE GAME ENDED, the crowd grew a lot thinner, though those that stayed were louder, drunker, and left bigger messes in the bathroom.

After a while, even they started to fade. Rardy passed out by the pool table and his friends dragged him out of there, one of them shooting Bob apologetic looks the whole way.

Bob glanced over at Eric and Nadia from time to time, still sitting at the same cocktail table, talking. Every time he did, Bob felt more and more diminished. If he glanced over there enough times, he'd vanish.

After four Stolis, Eric finally went to the bathroom, and Nadia walked up to the bar.

Bob leaned on the bartop. "Are you with him?"

Nadia said, "*What?*"

Bob said, "Are you? Just tell me."

Nadia, "Good God, what? No. No, I'm not with him. No, no, no. Bob? I show up at my house this afternoon, he's waiting in my kitchen with a gun in his waistband like it's *Silverado*. Says I gotta come with him to see you."

Bob wanted to believe her. Wanted to believe her so hard it could shatter his teeth; they'd shoot out of his mouth, spray all over the bar. He got a good look in her eyes finally, saw something he still couldn't fully identify—but it definitely wasn't excitement or smugness or the bitter smile of a victor. Maybe something worse than all of that—despair.

Bob said, "I can't do this alone."

Nadia said, "Do what?"

Bob said, "It's too hard, you know? I've been serving this . . . sentence for ten years—every fucking *day*—because I thought somehow it'd square me when I got to the other side, ya know? I'd get to see my ma and my old man, stuff like that? But I don't think I'll be forgiven. I don't think I should be. But, but I'm supposed to be alone on the other side *and* on this one too?"

"No one's supposed to be alone. Bob?" She put her hand on his. Just a second, but it was enough. It was enough. "No one."

Eric came out of the bathroom and worked his way up to the bar. He jerked a thumb at Nadia. "Be a hot shit and grab our drinks off the table, would ya?"

Bob walked off to settle a tab.

BY ONE-FORTY-FIVE, THE CROWD was gone, just Eric, Nadia, and Millie, who'd amble off to the assisted-living place up on Edison Green by one-fifty-five on the dot. She asked for her ashtray and Bob slid it down to her and she nursed her drink and her cigarette in equal measure, the ash curling off the end of her cigarette like a talon.

Eric gave Bob an all-teeth smile and spoke through it, softly. "When's the old biddy pack it in?"

"A couple minutes." Bob said, "Why'd you bring her?"

Eric looked over at Nadia hunched on the stool beside him. He leaned into the bar. "You should know how serious I am, Bob."

"I know how serious you are."

"You *think* you do, but you don't. If you fuck with me— even in the slightest—it doesn't matter how long it takes me, I'll rape the shit out of her. And if you got any plans, like Eric-doesn't-walk-back-out-of-here plans? You got any ideas in that vein, Bob, my partner on the Richie Whelan hit, he'll take care of you both."

Eric sat back as Millie left the same tip she'd been leaving since Sputnik—a quarter—and slid off her stool. She gave Bob a rasp that was 10 percent vocal cords and 90 percent Virginia Slim Ultra Light 100s. "Yeah, I'm off."

"You take care, Millie."

She waved it away with a "Yeah, yeah, yeah," and pushed open the door.

Bob locked it behind her and came back behind the bar. He wiped down the bar top. When he reached Eric's elbows, he said, "Excuse me."

"Go around."

Bob wiped the rag in a half circle around Eric's elbows.

"Who's your partner?" Bob said.

"Wouldn't be much of a threat if you knew who he was, would he, Bob?"

"But he helped you kill Richie Whelan?"

Eric said, "That's the rumor, Bob."

"More than a rumor." Bob wiped in front of Nadia, saw red marks on her wrists where Eric had yanked them. He wondered if there were other marks he couldn't see.

"Well then it's more than a rumor, Bob. So there you go."

"There you go what?"

"There you *go*." Eric scowled. "What time is it, Bob?"

Bob reached under the bar. He came back out with the ten thousand dollars wrapped in the bag. He unwrapped the bag, pulled the money out, and put it on the bar in front of Eric.

Eric glanced down. "What's this?"

Bob said, "The ten grand you wanted."

"For what, again?"

"The dog."

"The dog. Right, right, right," Eric whispered. He looked up. "How much for Nadia, though?"

Bob said, "So it's like that."

"Appears to be," Eric said. "Let's just all chill a couple more minutes, then get a look in the safe at two."

Bob turned and selected a bottle of Polish vodka. Picked the best one actually—the Orkisz. Poured himself a drink. Drank it down. Thought of Marv and poured himself another, a double this time.

He said to Eric Deeds, "You know Marv used to have a problem with the blow about ten years ago?"

"I did not know that, Bob."

"You don't have to call me by my name all the time."

"I will see what I can do about that, Bob."

"Anyway, yeah, Marv liked the coke too much and it caught up with him."

"Getting close to two here, Bob."

"He was more of a loan shark then. I mean, he did some fence, but mostly, he was a shark. There was this kid? Into Marv for a shitload of money. Real hopeless case when it came to the dogs and basketball. Kinda kid could never pay back all he owed."

"One-fifty-seven, Bob."

"The thing, though? This kid, he actually hit on a slot at Mohegan. Hit for seventeen grand. Which is just a little more than he owed Marv."

"And he didn't pay Marv back, so you and Marv got all hard on him and I'm supposed to learn—"

"No, no. He *paid* Marv. Paid him every cent. What the kid didn't know, though, was that Marv had been skimming. Because of the coke habit? And this kid's money was like manna from heaven as long as no one knew it was from this kid. See what I'm saying?"

"Bob, it's fucking one minute to two." Sweat on Eric's lip.

"Do you see what I'm saying?" Bob asked. "Do you understand the story?"

Eric looked at the door to make sure it was locked. "Fine, yeah. This kid, he had to be ripped off."

"He had to be killed."

Out of the side of his eye, a quick glance. "Okay, killed."

"That way, he couldn't ever say he paid off Marv and no one else could either. Marv uses the money to cover all the holes, he cleans up his act, it's like it never happened. So that's what we did."

"You did . . ." Eric barely in the conversation, but some warning in his head starting to sound, his head turning from the clock toward Bob.

"Killed him in my basement," Bob said. "Know what his name was?"

"I wouldn't know, Bob."

"Sure you would."

"Jesus?" Eric smiled.

Bob didn't. "Richie Whelan."

Bob reached under the bar and pulled out the 9mm. He didn't notice the safety was on, so when he pulled the trigger nothing happened. Eric jerked his head and tried to push back from the bar rail, but Bob thumbed off the safety and shot Eric just below the throat. The gunshot sounded like a slat of aluminum siding being torn off a house. Nadia screamed. Not a long scream, but sharp with shock. Eric made a racket falling back off his stool and by the time Bob came around the bar, Eric was already going, if not quite gone. The overhead fan cast thin slices of shadow over his face. His cheeks puffed in and out like he was trying to catch his breath and kiss somebody at the same time.

"I'm sorry, but you kids," Bob said. "You know? You don't have any manners. You go out of the house dressed like you're still in your living room. You say terrible things about women. You hurt harmless dogs. I'm tired of you, man."

Eric stared up at him. Winced like he had heartburn. He looked pissed off. Frustrated. The look froze on his face like it was sewn there, and then he wasn't in his body anymore. Just gone. Just, shit, dead.

Bob dragged him into the cooler.

When he came back, pushing the mop and bucket ahead of him, Nadia still sat on her stool. Her mouth was a bit wider than usual and she couldn't take her eyes off the floor where the blood was, but otherwise, she seemed perfectly normal.

"He would have just kept coming," Bob said. "Once someone takes something from you and you let them? They don't feel gratitude, they just feel like you owe them something more." He soaked the mop in the bucket, wrung it out a bit, and slopped it over the main blood spot. "Makes no sense, right? But that's how they feel. Entitled. And you can never change their minds after that."

She said, "He . . . You just fucking shot him. You just . . . I mean, you know?"

Bob swirled the mop over the spot. "He beat my dog."

CHAPTER 16

Last Call

MARV SAT UP THE street in his car, parked under the broken streetlamp where no one would notice him, and watched the girl come out of the bar alone and walk down the street in the other direction.

Didn't make a bit of fucking sense. Deeds should be out of there by now. Should have been out ten minutes ago. He saw movement by the window with the Pabst light and the light went off. But in the moment before it did, he'd seen the top of someone's head.

Bob. Only Bob was tall enough for his head to peek above that window. Eric Deeds would have had to take a running jump at that light chain. But Bob, Bob was big. Big and tall and way, way smarter than he let on most days and, fuck, just the kind of guy who could stick his Dudley Do-Right schnoz into things and mess them all up.

That what you did, Bob? You fuck me up here? You ruin my shot?

Marv looked at the bag on the seat beside him, the plane tickets peeking out of the front pocket like a middle finger.

He decided the smart thing might be to drive around to the alley, sneak in through the back, and see what was what. He knew what was what, actually—Eric had failed to close the deal. In a moment of desperation, Marv had even called his cell ten minutes ago and got no answer.

Of course there'd be no answer. He's dead.

He's not dead, Marv argued. We're past those days.

You might be. Bob, on the other hand . . .

Fuck it. Marv was going to drive around back, see what was fucking what. He put the car in drive, and his foot had just started to come off the gas when Chovka's black Suburban drove past, the white van on its ass. Marv popped the shift back into park and slid himself down his seat. He watched over the dash as Chovka and Anwar and a few other guys climbed out of the vehicles. Everyone but Chovka carried rolling duffel bags. Even from this distance Marv could tell they were empty, the guys swinging them as they walked to the front door. Anwar knocked and they stood there, waiting, the breath puffing white from their mouths. Then the door opened and they let Chovka go in first before following him inside.

Fuck, Marv thought. Fuck fuck fuck.

He looked down at the plane tickets—it wasn't going to do him much good to arrive in Bangkok the day after tomorrow without a dime to his name. The plan had been to leave with enough money that he could bribe his way over the border into Cambodia, work his way as far south as Kampuchea, where he figured no one would look. He had no exact idea why he figured no one would look there, just that if *he* were looking for himself, Kampuchea would be about the last place he'd expect to find him. The *last* place would be, like, Finland or Manchuria, someplace really cold, and maybe that would have been the best bet, the smartest play, but Marv had lived through so many New England winters he was pretty sure his right nostril and his left nut were permanently damaged by frostbite, so fuck going someplace cold.

He looked back at the bar. If Eric was dead—and it sure seemed fucking probable at this point—then Bob had just saved the Umarov organization as well as every syndicate in the city millions of dollars. Millions. He'd be a fucking hero. Maybe they'd tip him a security fee. Chovka had always liked Bob because Bob sucked up so much. Maybe he'd give him as much as 5 percent. That would get Marv to Cambodia.

So, okay, new plan. Wait for the Chechens to leave. Then go have a talk with Bob.

He sat up a little taller in his seat, now that he had a plan.

Though it occurred to him that he probably should have learned Thai. Or at least bought a book on the subject.

Whatever. They'd have one at the airport.

CHOVKA SAT AT THE bar and scrolled through RECENT CALLS on Eric Deeds's cell phone. Bob stood behind the bar.

Chovka turned the phone to Bob so he could see the number of a recent missed call.

"You know that number?"

Bob nodded.

Chovka sighed. "I know that number too."

Anwar came out of the cooler, pulling a rolling duffel bag behind him.

Chovka said, "He fit?"

Anwar said, "We broke his legs. He fit fine."

Anwar dropped the bag full of Eric at the front door and waited.

Chovka pocketed Eric's phone, pulled out one of his own.

The other Chechens came out of the back.

George said, "We pack the money into kegs, boss. Dakka will be by, he say, another twenty minutes with the beer truck."

Chovka nodded. He was concentrating on his phone, texting away like a sixteen-year-old girl during school lunch. When he finished texting, he put the phone away and stared at Bob for a very long time. If Bob had to guess, he'd say the silence went on for three minutes, maybe four. Felt like two days. Not a soul moving in that bar, not a sound but that of six men breathing. Chovka stared into Bob's eyes and then past his eyes and over his heart and through his blood. Followed that blood through his lungs, through his brain, moved through Bob's thoughts and then his memories like moving through the rooms of a house that might already be condemned.

Chovka reached into his pocket. He placed an envelope on the bar. Raised his eyebrows at Bob.

Bob opened the envelope. Inside were Celtic tickets.

Chovka said, "They're not floor seats but they are very good. They're my seats."

Bob's heart pumped again. His lungs filled with oxygen. "Oh. Wow. Thank you."

Chovka said, "I'll drop off some more next week. I don't go to all the games. There's a lot of games, you know? I can't get to all of them."

Bob said, "Sure."

Chovka read a message off his phone and began texting in response. "Got to give yourself an hour before the game to get there, an hour after because of the traffic."

Bob said, "Traffic can get bad."

Chovka said, "I tell Anwar, he says it's not bad."

Anwar said, "It's not like London."

Chovka was still texting. "What's like London? Let me know if you enjoy them, Bob. He just came in?" He pocketed his phone, looked at Bob.

Bob blinked. "Yeah. Right through the front door after I let Millie out."

Chovka said, "Put that gun in your face but you said, 'Not tonight,' eh?"

Bob said, "I didn't say anything."

Chovka mimed pulling a trigger. "Sure, you did. You said *pop*." Chovka reached into his inside pocket again, came out with another envelope. It flapped open when he tossed it on the bar, thick with money. "My father want you to have this. The last time my father gave money to someone? Whoo. You honorary Umarov now, Bob."

Bob couldn't think of anything to say but "thank you."

Chovka patted Bob's face. "Dakka will be by soon. Good night."

Bob said, "Good night. Thank you. Good night."

George opened the door and Chovka exited, lighting a cigarette. Anwar followed, pulling the roller bag of Eric behind him, the wheels bumping over the threshold and then again on the icy sidewalk.

WHAT THE FUCK WAS this now? Marv watched the Chechens exit the bar with one duffel bag that required two guys to lift it into the back of the van. He would have thought they'd have more than one bag. All that money?

He rolled down his window as they drove off and flicked his cigarette out onto the crust of snow by the hydrant. The cigarette rolled off the hard mound, rolled down the curb, and hissed when it found a puddle there.

Another thing he'd need to do when he got to Thailand— quit smoking. It was enough already. He went to roll the window up and saw a guy standing three inches away on the sidewalk.

Same guy who'd asked him for directions a few weeks back.

"Ah, shit," Marv said softly as the guy shot him through the nose.

"GO IN PEACE NOW to love and serve the Lord."

Father Regan made the sign of the cross and that was it— the final mass.

They all looked around at one another, the hardy few, the penitents and patrons of the seven—Bob and Torres, Widow Malone, Theresa Coe, Old Man Williams, as well as several people who hadn't been by in a while making return cameos and guest appearances for this, the final show. Bob could see the same numbness in all their faces—they'd known it was going to happen and yet, somehow, they hadn't.

Father Regan said, "If anyone would like to purchase one of the pews before they are sold for consignment, please call Bridie in the rectory, which will be open for another three weeks. God bless you all."

No one moved for a minute. And then Widow Malone shuffled out into the aisle and Torres was next. Followed by some of the guest stars. Bob and Old Man Williams were the last two out. At the holy water font, Bob blessed himself within these walls for the last time and caught Old Man Williams's eye. The old man smiled and nodded several times but said nothing, and they walked out together.

ON THE SIDEWALK, HE and Torres stood looking back up at it.

"When did you take your tree down this year?" Bob asked.

Torres said, "Day after Little Christmas. You?"

Bob said, "Same."

They nodded at each other and went back to looking at the church.

"Just like I predicted," Torres said.

"What's that?"

"They sold it to Milligan Development. It's going to be condos, Bob. Seculars sitting up there behind that beautiful window, sipping their fucking Starbucks and talking about the faith they put in their Pilates teacher." He gave Bob a soft, rueful smile and shrugged. After a minute he said, "You love your father?"

Bob looked at him long enough to see he was completely serious. "A shitload."

Torres said, "You guys were close?"

Bob said, "Yeah."

"Me too. You don't hear that a lot." He looked up again. "It was a gorgeous church. Sorry to hear about Cousin Marv."

"Carjacking gone bad, they said."

Torres widened his eyes. "That was an execution. A block and a half from your bar."

Bob looked up the street for a bit and said nothing.

Torres said, "Eric Deeds. I mentioned him to you once."

"I remember."

"You didn't then."

"I remember you mentioning him."

Torres said, "Ah. He was in your bar Super Bowl Sunday. You see him?"

Bob said, "You know how many people were in that bar Super Bowl Sunday?"

Torres said, "Last place he was ever seen. Then? Poof. Just like Richie Whelan. Ironic, since Deeds supposedly killed Whelan. Bodies getting clipped or vanishing all over the place, but you don't see anything."

Bob said, "He could turn up."

Torres said, "If he does, it'll probably be in a psych ward. Which is where he was the night Whelan disappeared."

Bob looked over at him.

Torres nodded several times. "True. His partner told me Deeds always took credit for the Whelan hit because nobody else wanted to and he thought it helped his street cred. But he didn't kill Whelan."

Bob said, "Will he be missed, though?"

Torres couldn't believe this guy. He smiled. "Will he be what?"

Bob said, "Missed."

Torres said, "No. Maybe Whelan wasn't, either."

Bob said, "That's not true. I knew Glory Days. He wasn't a bad guy. Not at all."

For a time, neither of them said anything. Then Torres leaned in. "No one ever sees you coming, do they?"

Bob kept his face as clear and open as Walden Pond. He held out his hand and Torres shook it. "You take care, Detective."

"You too."

Bob left him there, staring at a building, helpless to change anything that went on in there.

NADIA CAME TO HIM a few days later. They walked the dog. When it was time to go home, they walked to hers, not his.

"I've gotta believe," Nadia said when they were inside, "that there's a purpose. And even if it's that you kill me as soon as I close my eyes—"

"Me? What? No," Bob said. "Oh, no."

"—then that's okay. Because I just can't go through any more of this alone. Not another day."

"Me too," he said, his eyes closed tight. "Me too."

They didn't speak for a long time. And then:

"He needs a walk."

"Huh?"

"Rocco. He hasn't been out in a while."

He opened his eyes, looked at the ceiling of her bedroom.

She'd pasted star decals there when she was a kid and they were still there.

"I'll get the leash."

IN THE PARK, THE February sky hung just above them. The ice had broken on the river but small chunks of it clung to the dark banks.

He didn't know what he believed. Rocco walked ahead of them, pulling on the leash a bit, so proud, so pleased, unrecognizable from the quivering hunk of fur Bob had pulled from a barrel just two months ago.

Two months! Wow. Things sure could change in a hurry. You rolled over one morning, and it was a whole new world. It turned itself toward the sun, stretched and yawned. It turned itself toward the night. A few more hours, and it turned itself toward the sun again. A new world, every day.

When they reached the center of the park, he unhooked the leash from Rocco's collar and reached into his coat for a tennis ball. Rocco reared his head. He snorted loud. He pawed the earth. Bob threw the ball and Rocco took off after it. Bob envisioned the ball taking a bad bounce into the road. The screech of tires, the thump of metal against dog. Or what would happen if Rocco, suddenly free, just kept running.

But what could you do?

You couldn't control things.

About the Author

DENNIS LEHANE is the author of thirteen novels—including the *New York Times* bestsellers *Live by Night; Moonlight Mile; Gone, Baby, Gone; Mystic River; Shutter Island;* and *The Given Day*—as well as *Coronado,* a collection of short stories and a play. He grew up in Boston, Massachusetts, and now lives in California with his family.

MORE BY DENNIS LEHANE

SHUTTER ISLAND

In the year 1954, U.S. Marshal Teddy Daniels and his new partner, Chuck Aule, come to Shutter Island, home of Ashecliffe Hospital for the Criminally Insane, to investigate an unexplained disappearance. But nothing at Ashecliffe Hospital is remotely what it seems...

LIVE BY NIGHT

Dennis Lehane's epic, unflinching tale of Prohibition, the Roaring Twenties, and one man's rise from Boston petty thief to the Gulf Coast's most successful rum runner. Joe Coughlin enjoys the thrills of being an outlaw, but one fate seems most likely for men like Joe: an early death.

MYSTIC RIVER

When they were children, Sean Devine, Jimmy Marcus, and Dave Boyle were friends. But then a strange car pulled up to their street. One boy got into the car, two did not, and something terrible happened—something that ended their friendship and changed all three boys forever.

SACRED

A beautiful, grief-stricken woman has vanished without a trace. So has the detective hired to find her. So has a pile of money... Enter tough-nosed private investigators Patrick Kenzie and Angela Gennaro, who've seen it all. But this case leads them into unexpected territory: a place of lies and corruption.

GONE, BABY, GONE

The tough neighborhood of Dorchester is no place for the innocent or the weak—and now one of its youngest is missing. After pleas from the child's aunt, private investigators Patrick Kenzie and Angela Gennaro open the case, an investigation that will ultimately risk everything.

PRAYERS FOR RAIN

When Patrick first meets Karen Nichols, she strikes him as a woman untouched by tragedy. But six months later Karen leaps naked from one of Boston's monuments, and Patrick wants to know why. What he discovers is a sadistic stalker who methodically drove the woman to her death—a monster that the law can't touch.

A DRINK BEFORE THE WAR

A cabal of powerful Boston politicians is willing to pay private investigators Patrick Kenzie and Angela Gennaro big money for a seemingly small job: to find a missing cleaning woman who stole some secret documents. But this crime is no ordinary theft, and in Boston, finding the truth isn't just a dirty business... it's deadly.

MOONLIGHT MILE

In *Gone, Baby, Gone*, Amanda McCready was four years old when she vanished from a Boston suburb in 1997. In this sequel, Amanda is sixteen—and gone again. Haunted by the past, private investigators Patrick Kenzie and Angela Gennaro revisit the case that troubled them the most.

DARKNESS, TAKE MY HAND

Patrick Kenzie and Angela Gennaro's latest client is a prominent Boston psychiatrist running scared from a vengeful Irish mob. But an evil for which even they are unprepared is about to strike as secrets long-dormant erupt, setting off a chain of violent murders that will stain everything.

WORLD GONE BY

Ten years have passed since Joe Coughlin's enemies killed his wife, and the world has changed. Now the former crime kingpin works as a consigliere to a crime family, but success cannot protect him from the dark truth of his past—and ultimately, the wages of a lifetime of sin will finally be paid in full.

THE GIVEN DAY

Dennis Lehane tells the story of two families—one black, one white—swept up in a maelstrom of revolutionaries and anarchists, immigrants and ward bosses, Brahmins and ordinary citizens, all engaged in a battle for survival and power at the end of World War I.

CORONADO

In this short story collection, Dennis Lehane has compiled the best of his previously published short stories, as well as a story unique to this collection.

DISCOVER GREAT AUTHORS, EXCLUSIVE OFFERS, AND MORE AT HC.COM